Dead Man's Fury

Dead Man's War #3

Dan Decker

Grim Archer Media

Text Copyright © 2020 Dan Decker
All rights reserved.
Published by Grim Archer Media, a publishing imprint of Xander
Revolutions LC

This is a work of fiction. Names, characters, places, and incidents either
are the product of the author's imagination or are used fictitiously, and
any resemblance to actual persons, living or dead, events, or locales is
entirely coincidental.

For my wife.

Contents

1

To: General Gregory Seed
From: Brigadier General Forrest Brown
Log date: 00429.211-07:03:36

Re: Planet B24-X52745

General Seed,

We have found the missing lurker carriers. They are in orbit around planet B24-X52745 and are launching an invasion. We do not have any carriers close enough to respond to the situation in time, but SEP LurkerKiller and SRP Red Shot will be onsite in less than five hours.

A general alert has been sounded and our ground forces are preparing for the invasion.

General Brown

2

Jeffords muttered a curse as we watched the ships descend in the most awesome display of power I had ever seen, ripping through the atmosphere like a cosmic phenomenon that seemed to shake the world. Several of the large ships made me think of aircraft carriers from back on earth, only much bigger. There were hundreds of smaller ships that were dwarfed in comparison to the massive carrier ships but which were still of considerable size themselves, judging by how far away they were and how clear of a view I had of them. Whether large or small, they all looked like flying bricks. The largest were big enough to blot out the sun even without all the other smaller ships swarming around them.

They moved like giants across the sky.

It's more like a force of nature than an invasion, I thought.

The movies and televisions shows I had seen as a kid depicting alien invasions did not even come close to the power and horror of this singular moment. The world itself seemed to shudder in fear at their approach. It was as if the air was filled with electricity, of which the blaring camp sirens were only a muted part.

I had doubted whether the story about an intergalactic war was real—an unconscious part of me still believed that this could all be some twisted psychological drug experiment—but I could not escape the utter reality of it all, though my mind immediately tried to look for ways to do so.

I keep hoping that this is the worst drug-induced coma ever known to man, so I wake up to my family, but every time I turn around, this place gives me further evidence against that.

The atmosphere was filled with flame as the ships descended, several of the smaller ones broke away from the main convoy and headed our way while the rest continued in a direction that I pegged as northwest from our position, leaving behind contrails that made the horizon seem overcast. As concerned as I was about the ships headed towards us, I desperately wanted to know where the bulk of the invasion was going. They had led me to believe there was not much else on this planet, but that did not appear to be the case, judging by the sudden show of force that was largely ignoring us.

There was no way that they had sent that many ships just to deal with our lowly camp. The size of the invading force proved that there was a much stronger presence on this planet than I had been told.

"Camp Myers," Jeffords muttered under his breath.

Bingo, I thought. *Camp Myers won't be anywhere near as small as this.*

"How big is Camp Myers?" I asked.

The way Jeffords had emphasized the name Camp Myers made me think of something far more sophisticated than our camp, as if it were a headquarters of some sort.

Jeffords didn't answer and took off at a run.

I sighed as I watched him go. I had not had a moment of rest since coming to this insane planet. It was always one thing after the next. A part of me almost hoped for death, but then I thought of my little Ricky and my wife Ava. I could not surrender to such thoughts. I had to know if they had died several hundred years ago after long and fulfilling lives or if they were still alive or if it was something else altogether.

I had no baseline for truth, so I had to find my own.

Not knowing what else to do, I followed Jeffords, hoping that I could use the oncoming invasion to further prove myself, if not to him, then to Roth and anybody else who was in a position to help me understand what was going on here. The two ships that headed our way were coming fast. They had been some of the smallest in the fleet, but they were larger than any airplane I had ever seen back on earth.

And they kept growing in size as they approached.

I heard a high buzzing sound that I assumed came from the ships, but I was not sure about my assessment and feared that it was a weapon that was about to rain down destruction upon our little camp.

The camp sirens continued to blare, but as the ships approached, they became increasingly muted by the coming invasion to the point it sounded like the sirens had stopped working altogether even though I could still see the flashing lights.

Soldiers ran in every direction.

Up ahead, I saw Roth before she disappeared into a tent. Jeffords must have seen her as well because he headed right towards her. I did not know a lot about the chain of command around here, but I suspected he was not her direct report.

Sergeants didn't report to generals.

The tent she had gone into appeared to be the same command tent that had been uprooted by the grenling in my first meeting with her, only it had been moved to a different location since that time. It was still the same setup I remembered from that first day with multiple tents conjoined together to make a big meeting place within.

When I looked inside I saw several other soldiers who I assumed were officers. I was yet to see any sign of distinguishable rank on any of the officer's uniforms, I assumed this was to make it harder for our enemy to pick out our leaders. By the way they all carried themselves and ignored Jeffords when he entered, I could tell that they were all his superiors, except for the soldier who acted as Roth's secretary.

I did a double-take, looking her over, glad that she had survived my first encounter with a grenling. I had feared she died.

There was another woman with hair pulled behind her head who stood even taller than Roth, who herself was a tall woman. She glanced at Jeffords and did not bother to hide a disdainful look. She shook her head in irritation before turning her attention back to Roth.

I had entered too but made myself scarce by pushing up against the canvas wall, Roth gave me an unreadable look before turning to the others. We had not spoken since I had saved her life.

She had not given me so much as a thank you.

Not that I was expecting one, not from somebody like her.

"Sanchez," Roth said, looking at a fit man that was several inches shorter than her, but who towered over Jeffords, "what are you doing here?"

As I looked around the room, I remembered that I was taller than everybody. *And here I was hoping to shrink into the corner without being noticed.* It now felt as though everybody's eyes were on me, even though they all stared at Roth.

"All my soldiers are in place and we should have the big gun up and running in just a couple of minutes, sir. I thought I would make myself available in case you need anything else, sir."

The big gun? I had to refrain from shaking my head in utter amazement. *Why didn't they pull it out for the grenlings?*

"I gave you specific orders to get that gun going, what could possibly be more important than that?" Roth's eyes narrowed. "I don't hear it firing, do you? We could've taken down half of them by now if you would've got your act together."

I would have cowered under Roth's stare, but the man didn't even blink. He seemed to lack a sense of humor to go along with his brutish body.

"I wanted to see if you had any special orders, sir." His voice was stiff as a board.

"Kill as many of those infernal things as you can. Now get outta here!"

When the man moved to leave, I could tell Roth wanted to order him to run, but she just shook her head and looked at the tall woman.

"Benning, do we have any word on reinforcements?"

The woman frowned. "Everybody else is under attack as well. We have to go this alone."

"What's new?" Roth muttered, finally looking at Jeffords. "And what are you doing here, don't you have a team of fresh recruits to evacuate?" Roth stared at him, but I could tell she was thinking about me.

I wondered how it felt for her to be saved by me, somebody who had not even been here a week.

Jeffords snapped to attention, which apparently included fists at his side, something he had never taught any of us.

"Waiting for orders, sir."

Roth spoke through clenched teeth. "Standard protocol is to evacuate all recruits who have not yet been certified through Phase I. Unless you're further along than I anticipate, you should already know what to do." She threw her hands up in the air and looked like she wanted to strangle him. "What is it with you guys? The moment things start to get difficult, it's like all training goes out the window. I may have to find better officers." She let out a long and frustrated sigh. "Sergeant Jeffords, I just need you to get your men out of here. Can you do that? A man of your alleged experience should be able to handle that, or do I need to have somebody else do it for you?"

"With all due respect—"

"You already have the worst casualty count of any of our sergeants, I suggest you get going before your numbers look even worse. Get them out of here. Now."

Worst casualty count?

How many recruits has he lost?

I was not aware of any deaths from my team other than Winston, but we were only on our fourth day. Judging by the way Jeffords had acted after Winston's death, it had seemed as if losing recruits was something that happened all the time. Perhaps it was—Roth's words could be interpreted that way—but it was clear that there was a line and that Jeffords had passed it on multiple occasions.

Interesting.

"Yes, sir."

Jeffords grabbed me by the arm and pulled me outside, his face red.

3

I wondered as we ran if Jeffords was embarrassed because Roth had chewed him out in front of me. He did not even look at me from the corner of his eye, not even when I jostled him because I had to jump out of the way of a soldier who had appeared suddenly with a rifle pointed right at me.

I couldn't tell if it was because Jeffords' mind was somewhere else or if he was embarrassed. I was surprised by the determined look on his face and wondered if he was going to obey Roth's directive. Something about the way Roth had given him the order made me think that she had had trouble getting Jeffords to obey orders in the past.

Running is the last thing he wants to do right now.

I thought back to John Jeffs' psychological profile on earth. The man had been a coward who worked from the shadows, taking his victims in a way that made it difficult for anybody to tie them back to him. Even in his professional life, he had arranged things to avoid human interaction as much as possible. Jeffs had never had a girlfriend, and as near as we could tell, the only people he ever talked with were his victims.

What has changed between then and now?

I stifled a mirthless chuckle.

The answer was right in front of me.

As far as I knew, one's personality depended on the makeup of the brain. I suspected that this was part of what had happened to Jeffords.

I was far more aggressive here than I had ever been back on earth. Along with changes in the brain, it was also easy to attribute this to finding myself in a bigger body, which presumably had more testosterone than my last one, but there were any number of other factors that could affect my emotions. It was anybody's guess if their method of transferring people from one body to another brought along those same inherent personality characteristics without changing them, but judging by my limited experience, it did not seem likely.

I am still me, yet I am different from my former self.

I was a little more prone to anger and took risks, particularly physical risks, more readily. I still could not believe I had jumped off a cliff.

But couldn't my attitude just be explained by the situation?

Or maybe they pumped me full of chemicals at mealtime that made me more prone to aggression. They *did* want us to be soldiers, ideally going to fight without questioning orders.

Maybe Jeffords was not as sadistic as he had been back on earth because they had changed something about his personality. Perhaps this was why they could utilize him as a soldier. Maybe they had even taken precautions against such behavior.

I shuddered at the thought of a John Jeffs who was not a coward even though the evidence was right in front of me.

Jeffords pulled to a sudden stop and looked like he was trying to remember something while examining our surroundings.

"How are we going to evacuate?" I asked Jeffords in between breaths while scanning the horizon until I found the approaching ships. They were getting close. We had a couple minutes before they would be right over us.

I still didn't see any sign of the big gun, whatever that was.

If I were Roth, I would have been infuriated that my officers had been more interested in making contact with her, rather than carrying out obvious tasks, but perhaps she micromanaged them and could only blame herself.

Jeffords did not respond and burst into a run as he pulled up his watch and spoke into it. My watch buzzed and I heard Jeffords' voice coming from it a second after he spoke into his, creating a distinct echo that was whipped away by the speed of our movement.

"Meet at the south end of camp," Jeffords said. "Do not stop for anything. Everything you have is replaceable. You have five minutes." He pulled to a stop and looked back in the direction of the oncoming ships. "Make that four minutes. Time is short, and none of you are ready for this battle, the only thing we can do is retreat and let others handle it." He said this last bit with more than a degree of anger.

He did not look over at me as he burst forward, almost as if he were hoping I would just get lost in the shuffle.

He wants me to die in all this fighting so he can finally be rid of me.

A wild smile cracked my face.

It can't be easy knowing that I saved his life. I shook my head and chuckled at the irony. *The man who sent him away for capital crimes saved his life.*

Unless he had hidden weapons that I could not see, Jeffords was as unarmed as me. A group of armed soldiers ran by, heading in the opposite direction. When I looked back, I saw that the ships were now coming to hover overhead at the north end of camp. At first, I thought I was seeing transport ships, but after a second and third glance, I realized that what I saw were the actual aliens themselves and above them was a much larger ship. They resembled large insects, with heads like jaguars and bodies that closely resembled dragonflies.

They were jumping from an open bay in their ship.

They were also gigantic, easily fifteen to twenty-five feet long, and hit the ground like incoming missiles, sending soldiers and tents flying as they landed.

Jeffords had already gained fifty feet on me in the few moments I had turned to gawk, so I put on a burst of speed without further studying the creatures that were descending upon us like an ancient plague of gigantic man-eating locusts.

A shadow went by overhead, blocking out the scorching sun. I looked up to see another of the alien ships. It pulled to a stop while hovering a hundred feet above the camp. A door opened in the side, and one of the creatures jumped from the massive ship. Instead of falling like the others, wings stretched out from its back and it flew, far more smoothly than I would've expected of such a gargantuan creature.

I glanced back and realized the others all had wings as well, they had just made the hundred-foot jump as if it were nothing, probably aiming for surprise by hurtling themselves down into our encampment.

The flying monster above us roared as it swooped down, showing teeth that could have chomped me up in just a couple bites.

Did the infernal grasshoppers come all this way just to eat us?

Was this nothing more than dinner time?

Jeffords took a left to steer clear of the incoming monster. Just before I followed him, I caught a glimpse of a soldier being pulled from the ground and chopped in half by the creature's teeth. I sped by too fast to know if it ate him too. Soldiers fired their weapons into the massive abdomen of the beast as it went back up into the air. At first, I was cheered by the quick response, but as they fought, I realized that it was just like when they had fought the grenlings, this creature seemed to have a natural protection and bullets ricocheted off, flying in every direction.

Why don't our guns ever harm the enemy?

As I ran behind a tent while following Jeffords, I caught a glimpse of the creature's eyes as it came down in another dive—despite their insect-like appearance, their eyes did not look like insects—and something tickled my mind. I was unable to remember what it was but stopped thinking about it because I was too busy running to save my life. We were almost at the end of camp when Jeffords took a hard left towards a tent.

I was tempted to just go on ahead to meet up with the rest of my group, but I was curious about what could be so important to make him stop in the middle of all this. When I followed Jeffords into the tent, I was surprised to see a bunch of storage bins. I had just assumed he had gone into a barracks tent, guessing that Jeffords was taking something with him. He lifted up the lid of the closest crate and pulled out a rifle like the other soldiers had carried. It looked like something I might have seen back on earth, at least in concept, if not execution. It was recognizably patterned after a weapon that the U.S. Military had used. I believed the correct term was M-4 but could not be certain as I hadn't paid attention to such things.

Jeffords scowled when he saw that I had followed him. "What are you doing here, Anders? You're supposed to be heading to the south of camp as I ordered you."

"Give me a weapon, sir," I said with a straight face. Technically speaking, he was correct, I had disobeyed a direct order. I had not even thought about it because I just been following him while trying to understand what was going on.

He didn't hesitate. "Take two. The ammunition is over there. Did you ever fire a rifle back on earth?"

I shook my head. "Not since scout camp."

"This is nothing like that, and it is not as easy as the movies make it look, so I recommend you don't try to shoot any of the lurkers."

"Why haven't you trained us on them before?"

"They weren't scheduled for several more weeks. Do you have any more questions or should we get going?"

His sarcasm barely registered with me.

Several more weeks? In this environment?

With grenlings attacking every other day?

I shook my head and tried not to be irritated with the idiocy that seemed to surround me in this camp. Every time I turned around, I was convinced the decisions they made were geared more towards sending us to an early death than training us to fight in the supposed intergalactic war they had "recruited" us for.

I slung two of the weapons over my shoulder and found them light enough that I picked up another two, thinking I would pass out the extras to others of my team. It might earn me some goodwill, but I would not count on it.

The ammunition boxes were heavy. I hefted two of them and realized that I could probably take more if I had a way to carry them. After casting my eyes about, I found a bin of duffel bags and snagged one.

I threw in a bunch of the ammo containers and picked it up, or at least, I tried to. It was too much. I pulled out half of them, but it was still too much. Jeffords was already leaving and I did not want to get left behind. I took out another container and followed after Jeffords with the bag slung awkwardly from my shoulder.

I still didn't know how we were going to escape, but I assumed we would fly out using our anti-grav boots after Jeffords activated them. It still puzzled me that Roth had not seemed to know what I was talking about when I had mentioned this to her.

Just one more of the many questions that keep popping up.

Most of our training squad was there waiting for us. I was number six, that just left three stragglers. I turned to face the camp as Jeffords nodded at the weapons I held.

"Give your weapons to the others." Jeffords had taken an extra that he handed to Logan.

I unslung three of the rifles and handed them to the other men.

"All your weapons," Jeffords said. "I don't trust you. Scout camp, way back when, you say?"

"I saved your life. If you don't trust anything else, trust that."

Jeffords smirked. "You act like you did not hesitate. You wanted to leave me, hoping I would die. And don't forget about your act of disobedience just now. You were ordered to come straight here, but instead, you took a side trip."

I ground my teeth and was thinking about disobeying this order too when Jeffords got right in my face.

"Do it now or I will kill you right here, right now for treason. Nobody's going to blink twice if you die in all this, you stinky mangy maggot." He leaned forward. "I won't have to tell them I killed you, not in all this."

My insides turn to ice as I unslung the last weapon and thrust it out to one of Logan's cronies who gratefully took it but who did not say thanks.

I clenched and unclenched my fists as I watched the men remove the magazines from the rifles and load the ammo while Jeffords showed them how to do it.

Treason?

Jeffords is the traitor. Roth ordered us to retreat.

I fumed in silence, watching as the battle engulfed our camp. It had only been half restored since the battle with the grenlings, and the enemy insects were making quick work of what was left. By my count, I figured there were more than thirty of them, with more still on the way from the two ships hovering above us.

The enemy stood eight feet off the ground with their large wings protruding behind their backs when not in use. Their heads were all covered in the same scaly material as the rest of the body. While they resembled insects, the scales made me think more of reptiles.

Their snouts were short, with their two eyes buried deep in the sides of their head. We were not close to any on the ground, so we were not in any immediate danger because of all the fighting soldiers in between them and us.

Once the others had loaded their weapons, Jeffords ordered us all into a line. I went to my place at the front.

"All right, you filthy maggots," Jeffords said, yelling to be heard above the din of the battle. "This is your first taste of what it is we're up against. Fortunately, for all of you, General Roth has ordered you *not* to participate in this battle. The weapons you have are a precautionary measure only. Do not use them under any circumstance unless you must save your life. Although these might look like something you used back on earth, I assure you that there are some intricacies you will not understand with just a glance. Again, I cannot say this strongly enough, you are not to use these weapons unless as a last resort." He looked around. "Have I made myself clear, maggots?"

"Yes, sir," we all said.

I stared on with thin lips, trying to understand what he was doing. He was not evacuating us as ordered, and while he might have been waiting for the stragglers, I doubted it. Instead, he was making us watch the battle while giving us loaded weapons and expecting us to do nothing.

Giving them *loaded weapons.*

One of the monsters went down, but I did not have an adequate vantage point to see how it was done, perhaps there was a place where their armor was weaker so the bullets could penetrate and kill.

"These lurkers," Jeffords said, "are some of the deadliest creatures in the universe. Most of the soldiers you see out there fighting are going to die today. They caught us unaware, our soldiers are not properly armed and lack appropriate armor."

Then why aren't we evacuating?

Jeffords paced in front of us, his eyes angry. "Many good men and women are going down. These are not the slow and dimwitted grenlings you fought yesterday. These creatures are fast and mean. They will eat you alive in one gulp if given a chance. If you're still alive when you hit their stomach, they will start to digest you. It is not a pleasant experience. Word is that you can live for days before you finally die. I have seen soldiers rescued from the bellies of these beasts. All of them committed suicide rather than go on living."

He stopped right in front of me.

"Do you have a problem, Anders?"

I shook my head, doing my best to keep the simmering cauldron from showing.

"No, sir."

Jeffords stared at me for a long moment. "I don't like your attitude, soldier. It's time I punish you for your disobedience. Go take a lap."

I stared.

He wants me to run in all this? I shook my head. *Of course, he does.*

I was surprised but should not have been. For a moment there, I had thought Jeffords and I would finally be on the same team because we were facing a terrible foe. I had even hoped that we might start to come to terms with one another as we worked to extricate ourselves from the situation so we could live to fight another day.

Yet, he was once again trying to send me to my death.

"Are your ears not working? Do you not understand the words coming out of my mouth, soldier? You rotting maggot puke ball of flesh better get moving if you know what's good for you."

I took a step forward and Jeffords acted as if he thought I was going to punch him—the thought *had* crossed my mind—but instead, I pushed past him in a flat out sprint, resigning myself to face the battle empty-handed while the rest of my team evacuated in my absence.

4

To: Brigadier General Forrest Brown
From: General Gregory Seed
Log date: 00429.211-08:19:11

Re: Planet B24-X52745

General Brown,

Those recruits are not trained for a full-scale invasion. I suggest you order an evacuation as soon as possible.

I want the recruits to live. I don't care about the planet.

We can't afford the setback their deaths would bring.

Respectfully,

General Gregory Seed

5

I assumed as I took those first few steps that Jeffords was going to leave while I was running my lap. I hesitated and thought about turning around to argue my case but knew it would do me no good.

If I was going to survive the situation, I had to do it myself.

"Get going, soldier!"

I glanced back and saw Jeffords had pointed his rifle at me, his finger was on the trigger and he already had his head down on it as he aimed for me, heedless of the other recruits that looked on.

Nevermind the fact that we're under attack right now, I thought as I increased my speed, *you choose to aim your weapon at me instead of the enemy.*

A gust of wind nearly swept my hat off my head, which was saying something because it had managed to stay on through everything I done, all through my training exercises, and even those times I had jumped off the cliff into a ravine.

It secured into place after I jammed it back down. I couldn't remember what I had done to loosen it, but I didn't think of it again.

Jeffords would not have the slightest compunction against pulling the trigger. I hated how he always managed to put me in a situation where I had no choice but to do what he said because I would die if I didn't and I'd probably die if I did.

Several steps later, I was running as fast as I could, far faster than anything I had ever done before as I was eager to put as much distance between myself and Jeffords so I could find a way out of this mess.

The heat of the day had increased in just the short time since the alien invasion had started and sweat dripped down the back of my neck and shirt. The air smelled like death, but I wondered if that wasn't just my imagination.

I came around the tent and saw a group of dead men and realized the source of the stench.

I did not stop until I had gone around a curve of the camp and was no longer in Jeffords' line of sight and beyond the dead soldiers. After that, I slowed but still kept a healthy pace while I racked my brain, trying to remember the location of the tent with all the weapons.

Unfortunately, I had been so distracted by everything else going on that I had not paid attention to where we were going. I had assumed that we would evacuate, so I hadn't thought that I would ever need to go back there again.

That was my first mistake. I made an assumption. Never make an assumption, especially when Jeffords is around.

One of the lurkers landed a hundred feet in front of me.

I lurched to a stop on instinct but probably would have been okay to keep on going because it immediately hopped into the air and came down on top of a tent, crushing it like a tin can before it disappeared into the camp where I heard an uptick of gunfire.

I hesitated, trying to think of a better solution to this problem. Part of me wanted to cut through camp to see if I could bluff Jeffords on completing a lap, but something told me that he would know if I did and just punish me all the more, probably sending me to run multiple laps or order me to jump into a ravine again, while this time not engaging my anti-grav boots. He could get away with anything in this chaos.

It was an oversight for him to only order me to run one lap, probably because he had assumed that I would be killed on my way around.

I doubted he would make that mistake again.

He wanted me dead and was going to make sure it happened one way or another.

I looked suspiciously at my watch as I started running again, wondering what sorts of information it recorded about me.

I was perhaps a quarter of the way around the camp when a lurker came through a tent to my left like it was made of paper. This creature was a little smaller than the last and a darker shade of green.

A subspecies? Or just a younger version?

When it shifted, I caught a glance of its top and was surprised that it almost had a purple hue. Green all around and purple on top. I wondered if evolutionary factors had made it grow like that or if it was wearing some sort of protective covering.

I stopped just as my watch beeped, letting me know it was time to put on block. Stepping into the shadow of a tent, I pulled out my tube and applied it as fast as I could, leaving big smears on my face and hands.

The purple lurker was followed by several soldiers.

For a brief moment, the lurker studied me where I stood in the shadows. I figured I was a goner, even though it was still fifty feet ahead.

It opened its maw and roared but turned away and used one of its six legs like an arm, lunging forward to grab a soldier who was firing a weapon into its side. The lurker flung him back into camp like he was a ragdoll. I listened for the crash of his landing, but could not hear it through all the commotion. He had been high enough that I doubted he survived the fall.

Several more soldiers surrounded the lurker, maintaining its focus as their bullets pummeled its thick skin. Contrary to what I thought before, not every bullet was ricocheting off. Some were hitting their mark and penetrating, though there were still far more that bounced off. I started running again, careful to make sure the tube of block was secured in my pocket before I did.

It would be a terrible shame to survive all this and then die of a sunburn because I lost my block.

The lurker roared. Something about the way it stood and the sound it made tickled something in my mind again.

I've seen one before, but where?

Today was not the first time I had seen a lurker, though I could not say when I had. I certainly had never seen one on Earth and as near as I could remember, they had never shown us pictures of them here.

My heart beat faster than my feet as I ran, afraid that if the lurker in front of me didn't get me, another would. It picked up another man and tossed him like he was a toy.

The soldier was coming down in front of me, but at the last moment, he righted himself by activating his anti-grav boots and flipping upward in a maneuver that was both impressive and made my head spin. He stopped about ten feet above me while bringing his weapon to bear on the lurker and firing. A piece of spent brass hit the brim of my hat as I ran underneath him.

These lurkers make the grenlings look like child's play.

I was not about to play the hero today, particularly when there were others who were far better suited and trained to the task. I had no weapon and I just wanted to leave as we had been ordered to by Roth, even though I knew the chances of that happening were slim.

If I do manage to get back to Jeffords, he will tell me to do something else if he hasn't already left.

I needed another plan, but I couldn't think of what to do, so I continued to run, fearing that each step would be my last.

Once I was past the lurker, I looked back, just to make sure it wasn't following me. It had dispatched another of the soldiers, but several more had joined the battle. The man who had been in the air was back on the ground, firing at the creature.

Bright flashes came from the lurker—I could not see where they originated from—and all the men fell dead at once.

Stunned, I turned to run when the creature saw me.

It roared and chased after, the ground shaking underneath my feet as it moved.

Where did the flashes come from?

The lurker had no recognizable weapon. One moment those men had been alive, the next they had all been dead.

I look straight ahead at the empty wasteland in front of me.

I could not outrun it.

My only choice was to head back into camp and hope to distract it.

A thump came from behind that was accompanied by the wind of the lurker's wings. When I glanced back, the creature was in the air, heading straight towards me. Flashes of light hit the ground all around me as I ran for the closest tent.

Being in the air might have given it a greater vantage point, but it also drew gunfire from other soldiers, which was probably the reason why the blasts had missed me. Even though it was now almost directly overhead, it received fire from at least six different directions, judging by the tracers I saw flying in the air as I glanced back right before I ran inside a tent.

The ground shook as the lurker came down outside, roaring again.

The nearby gunfire went silent.

I was halfway through when the tent shook.

The metal frame was torn from the ground as light flooded in behind me where the lurker had uprooted the tent. The stakes dangled down as the lurker held it up with a leg that it once again used like an arm.

I dove under a cot and kept crawling forward, hoping that the creature might lose sight of me and would be drawn to other soldiers who were renewing their attacks on it after apparently shifting to have a better angle, if the gunfire I heard outside was any indication.

It would be nice to have a rifle. I shook my head. *Of course, I might've tried to fight instead of run and would be dead by now.*

The tent shook as I crawled out from under one cot and made my way underneath another. When the lurker roared, a ghastly rotten stench filled the tent. The wind picked up bits of sand and slung them into my face as I came to a tent wall. The cot right above me was torn away, its legs scratching my back as I lifted a flap of canvas and rolled underneath the wall to the chaos outside.

Another blast of sand hit me in the eyes and made it difficult to see as I stood and saw another lurker right in front of me on a collapsed tent. At first, I thought the lurker had crushed it, but when I saw how badly the frame had been damaged, I assumed it was the work of the grenlings. It had not even been twenty-four hours since the grenlings had been dealt with.

This lurker had its back to me, which meant I was momentarily safe. The canvas wall behind me began to shake as the lurker's claws reached underneath to lift it up. The canvas bulged at the top. I had mere seconds before the lurker would be free of the tent and I would once more be its main quarry. The way to the right was blocked by a crumpled tent. My only escape was to run past the lurker in front of me and hope it did not notice.

I dashed forward, wishing again for a weapon, because at the very least, I would have had a way to protect myself when it came down to a final stand, something that I assumed was moments away. I could have shot from the inside after it had eaten me, hoping to do more damage there than from without.

I studied the lurker as I passed, looking for its weapons, but did not see them. They had to be there somewhere, the only thought that came to me was that they were embedded in its flesh or that its armor was made to look like it was part of the creature and that the weapons were contained there. The lurker reared up on its back feet, giving me a view of a dead lurker in front of it.

How did they kill it?

I had to believe the weapons played a part, though from my present perspective they seemed to be about as useful as a BB gun against a lion.

I dashed into another tent as the lurker in the tent behind me tore free. I pulled to a halt to catch my breath, wondering if it had seen where I had gone. I shuffled forward through the tent, taking it as a good sign that it was not immediately ripped up. When I found another door, I was tempted to stay put and go to ground, hoping that the nearby lurkers would soon move on, but I knew in my gut that my best chance of survival was to get away from here as fast as I could and hope that none of the lurkers chased after me. When I darted outside I was once again on the outer edge of camp where I had been when the lurker had first taken an interest in me.

I stayed right up against the tent, controlling my breathing to not heave while also still trying to catch my breath as I waited to see if the lurker was coming.

I could not hear it.

I could not see it.

I listened for the sound of the lurker wings, but the chaos of the battle was so loud one could have been flying right overhead and I would not have known it.

As I crept back into the open, I feared that it was a trap. I did not make it more than five feet before I saw a shadow appear over me.

The lurker was perched like a bird of prey on the tent I had just come from, impossibly balanced on the top. Instinct, more than my eyes, told me that it was the same one. It opened its mouth.

I had no place to run.

The tent underneath it buckled and the frame collapsed. I sprinted forward, hoping to find another tent in which to hide. The next one was the tent the lurker had just uprooted.

There was a rush of air as the lurker took flight, once again attracting gunfire from all directions. It maintained its focus on me, despite all that. Did it identify me as a bigger threat because I was larger than all the other men?

Maybe these things thought size mattered more than brains.

Or more likely, it just wants a bigger meal.

I expected at any moment to feel its claws digging into my back before it pulled me up and bit off my head. Or perhaps it would just land on me, capturing me the way an eagle might have done a rabbit.

Maybe the fact I'm unarmed makes me more enticing.

The ground shook as the creature came down behind me. It roared again, but this was a different sound and I wondered if it was irritated by all the bullets coming its way. I did not understand why it had not just pounced on me, but assumed the gunfire was part of the reason.

I was not yet beyond the fallen tent, but feared it was about to lash out at me so I dove to the ground. As I landed, I felt something move in the air over me, and when I looked up, I saw one of its legs slashing above me. I crawled underneath the fallen tent, remembering how it had felt when I'd rescued Jeffords. My nerves had been rattled. My body had been pumping adrenaline through my veins, but it was nothing like what I experienced now.

I was filled with fear, but at the same time, I felt alert and was ready to do whatever was necessary to stay alive.

A moment later the canvas was ripped from off me. The lurker's leg tore into the ground right where I had just been, snagging onto a cot as it pulled back. The bottom of the cot glanced off my head as I scrambled to get underneath another while looking for a way to escape from this monster.

I stayed under the cots as much as I could but it seemed to pull them up just as I left the last.

Darkness enveloped me.

I wondered at first if I had died but then realized that the canvas had fallen down on top of me. It must not have been ripped all the way free. I no longer heard the lurker but kept crawling forward, fearing it was just moments away from getting me.

When I reached the other wall, I looked back and wondered if the lurker was gone.

Everything was quiet.

I feared it was a bad sign.

6

I waited for what felt like a long time as beads of sweat trickled down my head and into my eyes. Gusts of wind blew sand into my face from underneath the canvas tent. The noise of the battle came from all around me, reminding me of how I had sat on the floor of the brig and listened while the grenlings had attacked our camp.

Soldiers screamed in fury and cried in pain. Lurkers bellowed. I sighed when I checked my watch and saw that it had only been three minutes since I last saw a lurker. It seemed far longer.

Had the lurker moved on?

Or had it just been momentarily distracted because the soldiers outside the tent were firing their weapons at it?

I didn't think it was in the tent with me any longer, but I couldn't say for sure.

Was it a mistake not to run two minutes ago?

I shook my head. I didn't know what the right thing to do was.

I tried to listen past the sound of the gunfire, hoping to hear the noise of the big gun Roth had mentioned. I also listened for the distinctive sound of the special rifle I had used to take down a grenling. That particular gun had exploded shortly afterward, but it could not have been the only one in camp, right?

Even as I thought about it my heart sunk.

There was a reason why Roth had been the only one with one. I hoped to hear the sound of its report but heard nothing like it.

I strained my ears, trying to discern over the sound of the battle if there was a big gun. I still had not seen any evidence of the weapon Roth had sent the soldier out to man.

Maybe it has already been taken out.

Lurkers roared. Soldiers yelled. Soldiers screamed.

Soldiers died.

The lurkers were dying too, but it seemed to be few and far in between, judging by what little I could make out of the battle from what I could hear.

I tried pressing the buttons of my watch that would enable my anti-grav boots, having a half-cooked idea of using them to shoot into the air, but, of course, nothing happened.

What do you want to bet, I thought, *the moment that I left, Jeffords enabled everybody else's and they flew to safety?*

I turned at a noise behind, afraid the lurker had been there all along and was now coming for me—*I haven't moved, what did I do to give myself away?*—when another soldier sidled up, grunting with effort as they came out from underneath a cot.

It was a blonde woman, her hair was pulled back in a ponytail and she had a weapon.

"How long have you been in here?" I asked, immediately thinking afterward that I should whisper before realizing she probably couldn't hear me over the sounds of the battle.

"From the beginning. I saw the lurker chase you. Luckily, he did not notice me curled up in the corner." She coughed, something sounded off about her voice and I realized that she was sick or in pain. "I haven't felt right since the grenling attack. I was ordered to rest."

I nodded while looking her over and noticed she had a cast on her lower leg. "Are you able to move?"

"I think so, but I don't know for sure, this is the first time I have tried to get up since the grenling attack. This little invasion is bad timing. I was scheduled to go to the rehabilitator this afternoon." She snorted. "I don't think that's gonna happen now."

I frowned, wondering why she hadn't yet been into the rehabilitator when I had. My wounds had been much less severe than hers.

Had I been pushed ahead in priority because I had saved Roth?

"Can you stand?" I asked while carefully lifting up the canvas to allow in light so I could study her cast. It looked weak and temporary, nothing like what they would have used back on earth. I didn't think it would hold if she tried to walk. Given the superior ability of the regenerator, I supposed it made sense that they would not take the time to put on a proper cast. "Can you walk?"

"I don't know. Maybe. I haven't really tried."

"What do you know about these lurkers?"

"Is that what they're called, lurkers?"

I nodded, my heart sinking. I had been happy to have somebody else here because I was the least experienced soldier around. When I saw her weapon I had just assumed she would be more experienced and familiar with our situation.

"How long have you been here?" I asked in a small break in the noise.

"Since the battle started."

"You misunderstood me. I mean here in camp, since you woke up from dying."

"A little over a month."

"It has not yet even been a full week for me." I nodded at her rifle. "I take it you've been trained on their weapons."

She gave me a look as if I had just said something strange. "We did that the first day."

I grunted to cover my frustration and lifted the canvas so I could look out from underneath the tent wall. *Of course, she did that on day one. Was it just Jeffords keeping us back or was there some other reason we were not trained?*

I wanted to compare notes further, but feared we would die if we did not move soon.

"You know how to use your rifle?"

"I'm a good shot." There was something defensive in her voice that gave me pause, but only for a moment. I didn't know what it was and didn't care.

"In between the two of us, we have three working legs and one weapon. That must be good for something, at the very least we ought to be able to get out of here."

"You could give me a ride and I'll shoot anything that moves."

I had been thinking the same thing but had not wanted to suggest it because I was uncertain how she would take the idea, especially considering her response to my question about whether she could use the rifle. I was glad she had brought it up first.

"I think that is the only way we're going to get out of here."

I crawled forward, intending to roll out from underneath the tent but stopped when she grabbed my hand.

"Wait," she whispered right into my ear, her moist breath sending an involuntary shudder down my back.

I had missed it while we had been talking. There was a shadow outside, a large one.

My fingers were still underneath the canvas. I released my hold on the fabric and pulled my fingers back inside as carefully as I could, moving so slow that I felt like I was going to have a coronary from the suspense.

When the shadow moved forward it was clear the source of it was not human.

The lurker paused and I heard a noise I could only describe as a high-pitched snickering. I could not tell what caused it, but wondered if it wasn't the sound of the creature hunting by smell. There was just something about it that made me think the lurker was hunting.

I did not move a muscle and neither did the woman.

One minute passed and then it was two. When it finally moved on, I heaved a sigh of relief before I could stop myself.

"I don't know how we are going to survive." The woman's face was pale. "All my instincts tell me to flee, but how are we supposed to escape from those?"

"We will," I said, making my voice more confident than I felt, "no two ways about it." After we waited for another moment or two, I lifted the canvas and looked around. I was about to suggest we go around the other way because there was another lurker nearby. I clapped my mouth shut when I noticed it was not moving.

It was bleeding.

Perhaps our soldiers were not doing as bad as I feared

Two different colors of blood dripped out of the creature as it spilled onto the ground. There was a considerable mess of blood already surrounding it—gallons and gallons—seeping into the hardened sand like it was a dry sponge.

After several long moments without it moving or anything else coming to investigate my head poking out from underneath, I pushed out further and saw it was clear.

"Stay here." I pulled myself out from the tent and looked around, expecting a lurker to come out and swallow me whole.

The sun beat down on my bald head.

I curled my hand into a fist.

In all of the confusion I had managed to lose my hat, a fact I had not realized until now. I tried to think back to where I might have lost it, but could not remember it slipping from my head.

I was surprised, considering how the hat had stayed in place through almost everything I had done. It had not even slipped when I had jumped into the ravine. Maybe it had since been damaged, it had almost fallen off earlier.

I felt a distinct sadness at the loss of the hat because it was vital to my survival. I still had distinct memories of how the top of my head had felt that first day I had met Roth, but I could find a new one if we survived this.

I just hope my skin is not fried to a crisp before I do.

As I looked around I slipped out my bottle of block and rubbed some on to the top of my head just to be sure. I had gotten my head the last time I had put on block, but one could not be too careful on a planet like this. I put it on extra thick. I did not have a mirror but suspected my head looked like it was covered with white cream.

Far better than a burned scalp.

The lurker that had been chasing me appeared to have gone, an assumption that was not safe to make.

I got down on my knees and held up the canvas so the woman could come out. As she did I noticed she had a name tag on her shoulder. Her last name was Sampson. They had never given me or any of my other teammates a nametag.

Maybe they just wait until they know you're not gonna die during the first week.

When I offered her a hand, she looked at it suspiciously but finally took it. After I helped her stand, she put weight on her broken leg. I expected her to wince but she kept her face stoic, covering up the pain better than I expected. Now that I had a good look at the cast, I decided she could probably walk with it. It had seemed flimsy in the dark, but in the light of day it appeared to be sounder than it looked. The thin cast was covered with cords that gave it strength, almost like an exoskeleton.

"On second thought," Sampson shook her head with a rueful smile, "I think I can walk after all." She seemed relieved that I did not have to carry her. I was too and just hoped she could run, because we would have to. "Despite how they conscripted us, I can't say much bad about their technology."

I nodded, wondering if I might have finally found somebody who hated the situation as much as me. I wished I had the time to talk it over with her.

"Can you show me how to use the weapon, just in case I find another one or we get separated?"

"You aren't gonna rob me and leave me for dead, are you?" The challenge was back in her voice, but there was something else there as well.

Was it playfulness?

This was my first good look at her and I suddenly realized she was pretty. Her blonde hair was just barely long enough to cover her head.

I figured she was joking when a smile split her face. The behavior seemed foreign as nobody else here had once said or done anything humorous.

Unless you count Jeffords telling me to jump off into the ravine as a big joke.

At almost every turn I had been treated like I was an enemy. I was glad for something that reminded me of normal human interactions.

She held out the rifle, showed me how to disengage the magazine, and put it back in. "You pull back the slide to make sure a round is chambered, see? Down here is the safety. You fired weapons back on earth, didn't ya?"

I shook my head. "Not for a long time. Certainly nothing like this."

"Really." She frowned as she played with several strands of short hair on the side of her head. "I thought they only recruited ex-soldiers."

"You serve?"

"I was a Marine."

I snorted. "I was a lawyer. I was surprised when I awoke here. I thought maybe I'd gone to hell, but somehow this seems a little worse."

She chuckled. "You're the first non-soldier recruit I've met."

Now that was an interesting piece of information. John Jeffs had served as well, in the army, if I remembered correctly.

"Do you know John Jeffords?"

"No, but I've heard about him. I guess he's pretty hard on his group. I take it he is your drill sergeant?"

I nodded. "You could say that he's hard but I don't think that quite catches the full flavor." I hesitated, thinking of mentioning that he was a serial killer back on earth, but decided to skip over it. It was not my place and if I was serious about acclimating to this new world so I could figure out what happened to my wife and son, I needed to be careful of every single word I said, even to some random soldier in the middle of a battle like this.

"What are you doing here?" Sampson asked. "I heard over the coms that all new recruits were supposed to evacuate."

"I have not quite made it back to my team."

She accepted my explanation without further question. I did not want to explain that I had been sent to do a lap, because that would have come with additional questions and the last thing I wanted to do right now was to start saying bad things about Jeffords.

"Should we head out?" I asked.

She shrugged. "Better than staying here, I guess. My instincts tell me to run, but I don't think we can go far seeing as how we're surrounded by miles of desert. Let's see if we can find the regenerator so we can fix my leg."

I gave her a look, uncertain if she was joking or not.

"Or you can just carry me." Her face was still and then she smiled faintly.

7

To: General Gregory Seed
From: Brigadier General Forrest Brown
Log date: 00429.211-09:53:16

Re: Evacuation of Planet B24-X52745

General Seed,

I have ordered the evacuation but do not expect that we will save more than 70% of our recruits for the simple reason we don't have enough shuttles on-site to evacuate everybody. Some of the training encampments are equipped with shuttles, but most are not. Many of the remote camps are going to be left in a lurch.

I am looking at the situation with my team. We will continue to search for alternatives to save as many as possible.

General Brown

8

Sampson did better than I thought she would, even taking the lead for much of the way after she had warmed up. The cast she wore seemed almost as good as a new leg as it somehow managed to support her while keeping pain at a minimum. I was happy to see that she could hold her own and was glad that I didn't need to carry her. When we stopped for a break, I examined her cast and shook my head, marveling at how good of a job it was doing. In some ways it seemed as if her injured leg worked a little better than her other.

"That cast is holding up," I said.

"I have to be careful not to overextend my other leg." She gave me a thin smile. "That doesn't make the pain any more bearable. It still hurts. Why couldn't they have waited until this evening to attack? I would've had a brand-new leg by then."

The battle raged on.

We traveled between two rows of tents. This was similar to the route I had followed with Roth when we had escaped that grenling my first day. We moved along the side of the tents, opting to duck underneath the supporting cords, rather than move freely in the open.

Several lurkers flew by overhead, but they did not take an interest in us.

I did not seen the one that had been chasing me.

I just hope it's dead.

The moment we saw something moving we hid in the shadows until it passed.

The relative peace was unsettling, and had me jumping at nothing. At one point I spun around because of an uptick in the wind, afraid a lurker was landing behind us.

"A bit jumpy, aren't you?"

Sampson did not look back, making my face turn red, but I tried not to let it get to me. I still had much to learn about this place, and she had received training, even before coming here to this mad world.

Perhaps this was why a few moments later, when a lurker hovered overhead, I did not notice for several precious seconds. I was trying to prove to Sampson I was not jumpy and it almost backfired.

It was the smell that made me look up, the foul rotting stench was unmistakable and could only be one thing. The lurker was twenty feet off the ground and ten feet back, slowly moving forward but not looking at us. I froze, Sampson did the same.

I inched over until my body was pressed up against the canvas tent. Sampson positioned so that her rifle was pointed up. When the creature was directly over us, I slowly reached out and touched her shoulder because I feared she was about to shoot. She had not seen the way that bullets bounced off their skin. I did not want a ricocheting projectile to hit one of us.

She gave me a questioning look. I shook my head while mouthing the word 'ricochet.' She did not seem to understand at first, but after repeating it for the third time she gave a short nod. She angled her rifle so that if there were any ricochets, they would not hit us.

I held my breath expecting her to fire, but she did not.

We waited.

The lurker's wings were almost transparent. When in motion the wings were positioned like those of a dragonfly, buzzing just as quickly. The sand around us moved as if we had a helicopter flying just overhead, the movement of the wings created a low thrumming hum that grated at me in the same way it might bother a person to hear fingernails pulled across a chalkboard. Beads of sweat dripped down my face and into my eyes. I blinked, hoping the stinging would soon go away.

Each of the lurker's six legs looked like it was made of multiple joints, enabling the legs to move every which way. One of the creature's legs appeared to be broken and went off at what I assumed was an awkward angle.

The underbelly of the beast was pale white. Based on my experience with the grenlings, I had assumed that the lurkers were wearing an external armor, but now that I got a closer look, I realized that did not appear to be the case. There was a seamless transition from the underbelly of the beast to the armored scales it had on the rest of its body.

If the creature had not been right on top of us, I might have encouraged Sampson to take a couple of shots just to see if the underbelly was as resistant to bullets as the rest of its skin. I looked again for the weapon that was the source of the blasts that had nearly killed me earlier, but did not see anything that looked like a rifle.

The lurker did not move and hovered right above us.

Is it just toying with us in preparation to attack?

The creature's eyes still stared off in a different direction, so perhaps it was lying in wait to make an ambush and was just oblivious to our presence.

Those blasts had to come from somewhere.

The lurker's mouth?

Maybe it was a natural defense.

It seemed a stretch to think that the lurkers would have natural lasers, but I was starting to wonder if that was not the case when I finally studied a mass of moving tentacles just under the lurker's head. I had assumed at first this was a decoration of some sort but I could now discern arms with fingerlike tentacles.

The arms had hands, with three fingers each. What I first mistook as six-inch long claws, appeared to have two inches of finger and four inches of claw. The fingers looked like they could bend every which way as well. There were about a hundred of the fingers all told.

Several blasts flew out from the lurker's mass of arms, confirming my suspicion that this was where the weapons were located.

The wriggling mess moved out of the way when the weapons fired but returned right back to where they were before. The arms did not appear to have the same natural armor as the rest of the creature, but then why would they need it?

They were small and well enough guarded by the large looming head that they were not usually exposed to the gunfire coming from the defending soldiers.

If I'd had a rifle, I might have tried to shoot the lurker's hands just to see what happened, so perhaps it was a good thing that I was unarmed. I probably lacked the restraint Sampson showed by training the rifle on the beast, but not firing.

The lurker fired again and this time I clearly saw a small blaster that it held in one of its weird hands.

I started to count the passing time just to give me something to do to keep from losing my mind. Two minutes passed and then it was four, all the while the creature fired but did not receive much return fire. Several rounds bounced off its thick hide, but they might have just been strays.

The fact this lurker fired without resistance made me nervous, fearing that we were losing the battle. Just as I was starting to think of suggesting to Sampson that we might want to duck into the tent and come out the other side, the lurker zoomed away, moving so silently that it would bring death from above wherever it was going.

Sampson hesitated as if she were going to shoot, but then she put her rifle up.

I was drenched with sweat and it was not just coming from the sun's heat. My nerves were shot. I had no idea how we were going to get out of this situation.

"Hope you got a good look. You and I have probably just been treated to something that nobody's ever seen." Sampson chuckled darkly. "Not somebody that lived to tell the tale, that is."

Several minutes later we came to the end of the row of tents. Sampson gasped.

A moment later, I saw why.

The battle was over.

We had lost.

9

Sampson and I surveyed the scene in silence, each of us pushing into the side of the canvas tent to better hide in the shadow. It seemed like our little section of camp was the only place that still had tents that had not been smashed. Almost every other tent in camp was down. Lurkers roamed through, both on foot and in the air, every now and again receiving fire from one of our soldiers.

It was not long before they were put down.

The sight was disheartening, even though there was probably part of me that had been cheering against my captors.

I can't afford to think like that. Teammates. These people are my Teammates. I repressed a snort. *They might have conscripted me but they are my teammates still the same.*

The rat-tat-a-tat of a firearm started up and it was joined by more, apparently several of the soldiers had not gotten the message that the battle was over.

If I'd had working anti-grav boots, I would've been on my way out of here, that's what those guys should've been doing instead of continuing a losing fight.

Even more weapons joined and for a brief moment I hoped that we had read the outcome of the battle wrong.

No fewer than seven lurkers jumped in the air and converged on the willful soldiers, firing blasts of light from the lurker's puny little mess of arms.

The gunfire stopped.

The lurkers continued to fire for another couple of moments before they too pulled back. A fire had started in their wake, lighting up a fallen canvas tent as if it had been a piece of paper touched to a match. Four more crushed tents were soon burning. The lurkers did not seem concerned and went back to roaming through camp, looking for other survivors. The seven that had been in the air stayed there and they were soon joined by others.

"What we do now?" Sampson looked back at me.

"Are your anti-grav boots working?" I asked her.

She shook her head. "I'm not wearing them. The brace would not allow it. These are just regular boots."

I looked down and noticed that there were some slight differences between what she had on and what I wore, but it was not enough to make me think that the brace couldn't fit inside her anti-grav boot, but perhaps there was something I was missing.

We waited in silence, each left to our own thoughts.

"You don't have to stay with me," she said at last. "Activate your boots and go."

"I wouldn't leave you even if I could." I offered her a lame smile. "My boots don't work right now, they've been disabled." I hesitated. "They are still training us on them." I almost asked if they had deactivated hers during training, but refrained because I needed to keep us focused on getting out of here.

I looked at my watch and saw we had been stationary for almost two minutes while we had taken in the total desolation of the camp and the lurkers' efforts in eradicating survivors.

The lurkers were still going from tent to tent looking for any stragglers. Every now and again blasts of light would leave their mess of tentacles and they would put down the stragglers. It was just a matter of time before they started working on our section of camp. I didn't know what else to do, but clearly staying here was not going to keep us alive.

Our camp had been set up in the middle of nowhere, making it virtually impossible to escape. If we tried we would be sitting ducks for the lurkers. We would not get far before a lurker found us and took us out. If we'd both had working anti-grav boots, it might have been a different situation, but still, I would not have been willing to take a bet on that. I had not tested the capabilities of my boots and did not know how fast we could go. My instincts told me that the lurkers would be faster.

"Where are your boots?" I asked as quietly as I could while keeping a close eye for approaching lurkers.

"Back in my tent." She nodded towards the middle of camp. "Over there."

I covered my surprise because I had expected her to point back the way we had come.

Why wasn't she in her tent?

"If we found somebody else's boots would they work?"

I had not seen any human corpses yet, but the camp would be littered with them. It wouldn't be too much effort to steal some from the dead and give them to her. I could take some too.

"A nice thought, but no, the boots are keyed to the watch, and the watch is keyed to the person. That was one of the things they told us on our first day. You must not have paid very good attention. Didn't you say you were a lawyer back on earth?" She gave me a curious look as if she was going to say more, but then shook her head.

"We don't have long," she said instead. "Try your boots. Maybe they will work."

I hesitated and was about to argue but it was a simple request and it didn't hurt to check. I pressed the middle button on the left and the top button on the right, but my boots still did not work. In the back of my mind I heard Jeffords laugh, thinking he would be quite satisfied if he knew of my current predicament.

The lurkers were now all in the air and I was starting to hope that they were about to leave and we would be spared from having to figure out how to survive them.

A ship rose from the south end of camp. I didn't know where it had come from, it certainly had not been there before.

It rose quickly.

"That's no lurker ship." Sampson took a step forward and growled. "That could have been our way out of here."

"I was over there earlier and saw nothing like it."

"Didn't you say you were headed south?" Sampson asked me. "Why did you start there and then come here if that's where you wanted to be in the first place?"

"Long story."

"If you say so."

I could tell that she was now starting to wonder about me. Something in the way she acted told me that if she had an opportunity to flee, she wouldn't hesitate to leave me behind.

Had the ship been buried under the ground? Was that why Jeffords had ordered us to evacuate to the south?

The ship moved fast, but the lurkers were faster.

It was several hundred feet in the air by the time one of the lurkers caught up. Instead of firing its blasters the lurker actually latched onto it with its clawed feet. Ten seconds later there were five lurkers.

Twenty seconds later, ten lurkers.

Thirty seconds later, more than twenty. Not all of them had a place to grab hold of the ship, so some watched while others pushed their way in.

The ship's engines increased in power, but the combined wings of the lurkers were stronger.

They forced it down.

I watched transfixed at the scene, wondering if I would have been on that ship if Jeffords had not ordered me to run a lap.

Was Jeffords in there with the other soldiers from my group? Was Roth in there?

I had a hard time believing she had been killed during all this. I looked at my watch and tried to remember what time the invasion had started.

I gasped when I figured it out.

Has it only been thirty-eight minutes?

Perhaps Jeffords had been hoping to evacuate but had not had the opportunity. If the ship had been hidden in some underground garage, they should've waited for the lurkers to go.

Or at least come up with a distraction.

I thought back to the pocket of gunfire that had been dealt with minutes before, and wondered if maybe that had been set up as a distraction but had been handled faster than they figured.

More and more lurkers joined those who were forcing the ship down, hovering if they couldn't contribute.

Piercing sounds came from the group of lurkers.

"Is that a weapon?" I asked.

Sampson shook her head. "I don't know. I've never seen that ship before."

"It's a screaming lurker," I said, resisting the urge to point and realizing that I had spoken a little too loudly. "The ship is firing at it."

A blast from the ship hit the lurker again and it cried out in alarm. It was a soul wrenching high-pitched sound that made my skin crawl.

A moment later, the lurker at the front of the ship fell out of the sky and the ship suddenly lurched up, but not for long. Several more lurkers attached, staying clear of the weapon that had killed their fallen comrade.

They were fifty feet from the ground when the bottom of the ship blasted open and soldiers dropped out.

Two, four, six, ten, twenty.

All were caught by their anti-grav boots and fled in different directions. Several of the lurkers left to chase the runners, but the majority stayed to make sure the ship was pushed down. By the time it was to the ground, I'd seen no fewer than forty people flee the ship.

Lurkers chased the fleeing soldiers. Several had been caught right away, but others had already made it more than a mile.

Hoping against hope that my boots had been activated as well, I pressed the buttons, but still nothing happened. I ground my teeth. Even if my boots had worked, I didn't know what I would've done about Sampson.

I could not leave her. I might have tried to take her with me, but didn't think that would work very well. If those runners were to have any chance at all, they needed every bit of speed they had.

I leaned toward Sampson. "Now is the time to run while they are all distracted by the others!"

"But where would we go? The nearest place to hide is miles away. The lurkers will have dealt with all of them before then."

If both of us had anti-grav boots, or even if mine had just worked, we could have done something more than just watch the other soldiers die.

A lurker that had been hidden from our view hopped from the ground, grabbed a straggler that had been flying away, wrapped its leg around it, and tossed it like it was a worn-out doll. The anti-grav boots still worked and slowed the man's descent, but the lurker followed, firing its blasters.

I realized it was Logan when the body hit the ground fifty feet away from us.

His face was then blasted into oblivion by the lurker.

Sampson looked on without any sign of squeamishness. I did not look away, but my stomach wrenched.

Logan had been my enemy but it was difficult to watch him die in such a fashion.

He was recruited against his will too.

Several soldiers still glided away, going as fast as the anti-grav boots could take him.

The lurkers were faster.

Perhaps it was fortunate that my boots had not worked, because the lurkers hunted them down with ease, even those who were miles away. The anti-grav boots, while nice and seemingly fast, probably did not go faster than maybe fifty or sixty miles an hour, judging by how fast the soldiers flew and how quickly they were caught.

Perhaps it was just the limit of how fast they could go and maintain control. Maybe the limiting factor was that they did not have goggles to protect their eyes. Regardless, these lurkers flew like they'd been born flying and caught every single one of them.

A little dot in the distance disappeared as a lurker converged on it and destroyed it.

I opened my mouth, intent on suggesting to Sampson that it was time for us to use the distraction the ship had caused to take refuge in one of the tents that had already been searched when a lurker appeared overhead.

A blast ripped into Sampson, nearly severing her in two.

I dove and crawled under the tent as fast as I could.

10

I waited to die.

My heartbeat was in my ears. Every breath in my body was labored as the terror rolled through me. I could hear the final gasps of Sampson from where she lay on the ground, separated only by the mere canvas of the tent.

The low-pitched sound of the lurker's wings was all I could think about, like nails on a chalkboard, it moved up and down my back, making me want to cover my ears, so I did not have to experience it any longer.

But then it was gone.

I had expected the lurker to come after me, but it had left.

Had it not seen me?

My first thought was that this was a trap, but why would the lurker go to the effort of doing that when they had already won the day?

It could've just ripped off the tent and blasted me until I died.

That's what I expected it to do.

I looked at my watch and told myself I would not move for a full two minutes. I had been dead set on moving to another tent that I'd seen a lurker already examine, but was not so sure that was the right move any longer. I also didn't think I could stay one more minute in this camp than I absolutely had to.

When two minutes passed, I rolled to the wall and carefully lifted the canvas by no more than an inch to look outside. It did not look like there was a lurker's shadow above me, but I still waited.

The lurker had apparently been satisfied by killing Sampson. It was difficult to not look, and when I did, I did not focus on it.

I hadn't known her for long but I'd already liked her. She seemed a decent woman. It was a shame for her to have died so easily after both of us had survived the worst part of the battle.

Taking a deep breath, I lifted the canvas up so I had a clear view of the surrounding area. Once I was certain it was clear I rolled out and looked around. There was not a lurker nearby. Several flew in the vicinity, but they did not come my way.

They were leaving camp.

My first thought was to get Sampson's rifle, but it had been destroyed in the blast. The muzzle had been warped and twisted beyond any usability.

I dislodged the ammo magazine and put it in the pocket of my jumpsuit. It was better to have something than nothing.

Maybe I would find a rifle somewhere.

The smell of death threatened to make me empty my stomach as I crept forward to examine the camp.

I looked over at Logan's body.

Had he really been in his teens?

That was a shame too.

I didn't know what happened to us after we died here, but Logan shouldn't have had to experience what he went through. When I thought of how he had taunted me the night I had been put in the brig, part of me felt he had got what was coming to him but I pushed the thought away and did not let it enter again.

Jeffords' body is probably out there as well.

I crawled forward until I was at the edge of the tent, and looked around. A pillar of smoke came up from the shuttle the lurkers had forced to the ground. It looked like the engine had lit several tents on fire.

There were now two fires burning in camp.

I moved into the open, expecting a blast to hit me, but the lurkers were gone.

I spun, looking in every direction until I remembered that the main force had gone northwest. The last lurkers I had seen had gone that way. I ran to the west side of camp, heedless of the danger, and before I reached the edge I saw that the lurkers were all flying northwest.

Most were already far enough away to just be dots on the horizon.

I had survived.

11

To: Lieutenant General John Lincoln
From: Brigadier General Katrina Roth
Log date: 00429.211-10:17:23

Re: Package Request

General Lincoln,

Can you assure me that the package has been evacuated?

Brigadier General Katrina Roth

12

I let the relief wash over me for longer than I should have. I had survived, against impossible odds I still stood when so many others around me had fallen. I did not know how, but I had Jeffords to thank, at least in part. If he had not sent me to run that last lap, I would have been on the ship.

His spiteful act had saved my life.

At least until I die of thirst or hunger.

My first order of business was to find a weapon. I didn't know what else could come at me, but I suspected it would not be long before I needed to defend myself.

Grenlings. Lurkers. Crocs.

Or something entirely new I had not yet met.

What I really wanted was Roth's weapon. It had exploded and nearly cost me my life, but I wanted it anyway.

Despite all the dead, I had a difficult time finding a working weapon. Most of their rifles had been destroyed. The majority of the barrels were broken.

I felt like a thief as I went from dead soldier to dead soldier. I also checked the tents I passed for the supply depot we had stopped at earlier. I didn't find it.

I pilfered a backpack from a corpse and filled it with all the ammo I could carry.

When I finally found something that looked like a working weapon, I dislodged the magazine, pulled back the slide, and looked through the barrel. Relief flooded into me when I could see light coming through the other side.

There's only one way to know for sure.

I rammed the magazine back in, slid a round home, made sure the safety was off, and aimed at the horizon. I considered taking a potshot at one of the lurkers, but decided against it. I did not know how powerful the bullets were, but the last thing I wanted was to have a mad lurker coming back to hunt me. Instead, I faced the opposite way and aimed for a cliff in the distance. When I pulled the trigger, I expected recoil as I fired the bullet but there was none.

The gunshot was comforting.

For the first time since coming here I had a loaded weapon, even though I barely knew how to use it.

My next order of business was to find something to drink. All the activity had left me parched and I knew that if I did not find water soon, there would be little need to do anything else.

Water, then food. I touched my bare head. *And a hat.*

The camp had been destroyed, but I still found the mess tent.

It was crushed, like almost all the other tents, but using a knife I had taken from a dead soldier, I cut into the canvas and began searching around inside.

The attack had commenced right before breakfast, so I wasn't surprised to find large covered vats of food that were still in the warming trays, most had been overturned but a couple still stood. After rummaging around, I found a plate and loaded up some food. The juice dispenser was on its side and when I pressed the button it didn't work. Anxiety started to well up inside of me, but it turned out I need not have feared because I was strong enough to put it upright, something I could not have done in my former body.

When I pressed the dispenser button this time, I was rewarded with a mugful of juice. I downed it and then did two more, just in case. I wished for something to carry more, but as I did not have that option, the next best thing was to make sure I was as hydrated as possible.

After I had eaten the food, I went back outside and felt better for having refueled.

I felt bad stealing from the dead, but that did not stop me from pilfering a hat. It seemed small at first, but when I put it on my head it expanded to fit me. It felt so good to have proper protection from the sun again that I almost whistled aloud.

A glance at several nearby corpses kept me from doing that.

I next went to the south side of camp to figure out where the ship had come from.

It could not have been hidden in a tent, which meant it had come from someplace else. The only logical conclusion was an underground hanger.

I paced back and forth, trying to find the garage while wondering why the transport had been kept hidden.

Perhaps to keep recruits from trying to escape?

The ground around us was unstable, so it seemed futile to bury a vehicle.

I looked around where I stood and tried to get my bearings.

When I had originally awoken in this camp, the place where I now stood had probably been in the middle. The new ravine was several hundred feet south of me.

The more I thought about it, the more convinced I became that there was an underground garage.

I might find another ship if I could get inside.

To go where?

I dismissed the thought. One thing at a time. I needed a way to flee before I could do anything else.

I idly pressed the buttons of my watch to see if it would activate my anti-grav boots, but nothing happened. I would continue to check just in case something changed. I did not expect it to, but it would be a shame if I died with working anti-grav boots because I had not thought to check.

Try as I might I could not figure out where the ship had come from, so I wandered away to give my subconscious time to work on the problem.

The transport ship's engines were still going—even though it had been crushed by the lurkers—but not as powerfully as before. I approached from the front where it had been smashed flat. I had thought about checking for survivors but saw now that would be impossible

A vain hope had formed that I might be able to use the ship to fly out of here, but it would never move again.

Something whizzed by my head.

I spun, thinking it had just been a bug, but then I saw a man in the middle of camp with a rifle aimed at me.

As I dove I saw the flash of a firing muzzle.

The bullet grazed my shoulder as I landed.

13

I rolled, heedless of the pain in my right shoulder as it contacted the hard-sandy ground. Bits of sand dug into the wound making it smart all the worse, as if salt had just been rubbed into it. When I looked up I that saw that the man who had shot me was now coming towards me.

He was short and had a distinctive walk.

I knew him very well.

Jeffords.

Acting more on instinct than actual thought, I rolled my rifle off my shoulder and pulled the trigger. He went for cover.

He didn't expect me to know how to use a rifle.

Thank you, Sampson.

My watch beeped, signaling it was time to put on more block.

The only thing Jeffords ever told the truth about is the need to put on block, I thought, remembering how he had told us that even if we were taking fire, we should stop to put it on.

I knelt. I brought my rifle up and fired again in Jeffords' general direction, bracing my arm on my side to improve accuracy.

Both shots went wild.

I focused on the spot where he had gone down—it was a flattened canvas tent—and switched the lever on my rifle to burst and fired twice more, sending a handful of bullets at him. I dashed forward until I was back in camp, firing another burst as I ran, and then went down behind a flattened tent to catch my breath.

"We both know how this is going to end," Jeffords yelled, it sounded like he was about fifty feet away. "We both know you have no training. If you make me come find you, I will make it as painful as possible. If you stand up now, it will be over in just a moment."

"Was this why you didn't train us, to make it easier to kill me?"

I pulled out a knife and slit a hole into the half-collapsed tent I was using for cover and slipped inside, intending to go to the other side to set a trap for Jeffords.

I was surprised to see it was the medical tent where I had first awoken, perhaps I might have recognized it if it had not been crushed. I crawled to the far side and waited, hoping Jeffords would talk again.

He must have seen what I had done, because I could hear him walking, bits of sand crunching under his feet as they impacted the hardened sandy ground. He moved carefully.

I had planned to cut a hole in the canvas, but could not do that now without him discovering my location.

I should have just left him to die in the battle with the grenlings.

When I looked at my watch I remembered that I needed to put on block. After laying my rifle carefully beside me, all while moving as quietly as I could, I pulled out the bottle and applied it to every exposed square inch of my body, even removing my hat to make sure I got the top of my head.

"I'm glad you chose the hard way," Jeffords said. "I've been looking forward to making you pay for everything you've done to me."

I finished with the block and slipped it back into my pocket. I picked up my rifle and waited. The canvas was about two feet over my head. My best move was to go on the offensive and kill him outright the first chance I had.

"Have you figured it out yet?" Jeffords said even louder. "You know I am John Jeffs, don't you? You tried to pretend like you didn't figure it out, but you and I both know you're not stupid. You put it together and that's why you made that foolhardy leap off into the ravine. Come on out and face me like a man. You were a coward to put me behind bars. You should have just taken me out and shot me. Or tried to hunt me down yourself so we could face-off man-to-man. Instead, you hid behind the justice system."

I controlled my breathing as I thought of my wife and son.

My initial instincts were to hunt down Jeffords, but perhaps that was the wrong thing to do, even though the moment seemed to make it imperative.

When I finally got to civilization, or when others came looking for survivors, would they believe Jeffords had just died from friendly fire?

Maybe I could find a lurker weapon on a corpse and make it look like he was killed with that.

I still had no idea of my captor's present level of technical capabilities. Even though it seemed like we were alone and far away from anybody else, it was best to assume that whatever I did here would get back to the higher-ups.

A moment at the crossroads. Do I want revenge or to find my family?

I ground my teeth, wanting to figure out a way to do both, but I knew so little that I was not willing to take that risk.

I needed to find a way out while leaving Jeffords alive if I could.

I tried the buttons on my watch but my anti-grav boots did not engage. A moment later I was glad they had not, because that might have given away my position.

I'm too wound up.

I have to think this through.

"I missed on that first shot, you know that, don't you? I wanted to give you a sporting chance. Something you never gave me back on earth. It was the fair thing to do. It was the right thing to do."

He was closer now, perhaps just right outside the tent.

I controlled my breathing, making sure each breath was as shallow as I could possibly make it. The seconds seemed to take forever as a gust of wind blew through the tent, lighting upon my sweaty face and giving me a breath of fresh air.

Bullets cut through the canvas right in front of me.

I slid backward as silent as I could while wondering if I had somehow given away my position or if he had just seen the movement of the wind and assumed it was me. Either way, I needed to move fast. I moved through the crushed tent as more bullets came in, still focused on the spot where I had just been.

Can he track me?

I hated to part with my watch because I needed it at night, but maybe I had to, at least until I was safe.

My hand moved down to the latch, but I hesitated.

I didn't know that my watch had given me away. It might have just been the wind and a lucky guess that made Jeffords pick that spot. I needed more evidence before I ditched the one tool that I knew kept me alive at night.

I continued my crawl through the tent while my wounded shoulder screamed at me. Slowing my pace as much as possible, I worked my way towards the regenerator room after I got to what had been the hallway. The regenerator had been knocked onto the floor and crushed, almost as if the lurkers knew what it was for. It was not going to be in working order anytime soon.

Poor Sampson. Things might've gone different for her if she'd been prioritized.

I was soon at the end of the tent, right by the exit.

"You're still alive," Jeffords said. "Want to know how I know? I can see your heartbeat. Come out and take your punishment like a man. It's time for us to end this."

14

He knows that I'm still alive, but does not know my exact location. It appeared that there was something to my instinct to suspect my watch. I thought again about taking it off but waited, deciding I might want to fake my death after another round of bullets.

"Come out, come out, wherever you are!" Jeffords fired another burst into the tent, but it was on the other side and I was in no danger.

I slid out the exit, feeling like I was moving at the speed of an ant. Once I was outside, I laid where I was as I brought up my rifle, intent on jumping up and firing a shot at him the next time he spoke, trusting my ears to pinpoint his location. I clicked the selector back to single fire, both to preserve my ammo and to mitigate the risk of killing him by accident.

I would not kill him, only to have them not believe me afterward. He could say whatever lies he wanted when they came, but if he was alive, they would have very little reason to kill me too.

"What if I told you how to get back to your wife and son? Did you know that I can check on them?"

The more he spoke the more assumptions I started to make, which was dangerous. As much as I wanted to infer that this meant they did not know I had found the Bible, I could not afford to take that risk.

I have to assume they have seen everything I've seen and can even read my thoughts.

Jeffords might not have that capability, but somebody here probably did.

If they want to play God, why not act like Him too?

"I'll make you a deal—"

I sprung up, aimed high and fired. Jeffords still had his gun aimed at the middle of the tent, so I took him off guard. If it had been my purpose to kill him, I could have easily done so. My bullet sent him down to the ground and now our positions were reversed.

I stayed up.

He was on the other side of the tent across from me. I could no longer see him but knew exactly where he had gone.

As the seconds ticked by, I could hear sand and gravel moving as he crawled on his belly. The wind added to the noise, making it difficult to know which direction he was going.

"Jeffords, how about we throw down our guns and we end this man-to-man? You suggested that earlier, seems like a good idea to me."

I moved six feet to the left, careful with each step to not make any noise to keep him from knowing what I was doing. I had just assumed he would pop up after I spoke but he did not.

"If I thought I could trust you, I would do that but I figured out what you were when you put me in jail. You're a lying, thieving maggot who doesn't deserve the fair shake I've given him. No, the only way forward is to finish this little game of ours. Only one man is walking away today."

I kept moving. I paused when I got to the corner of the tent and could have sworn I saw the tip of his hat for just a moment. My next several steps were done slowly as I waited for Jeffords to take a shot at me.

The sun was now at its zenith and it must have been at least one hundred and twenty degrees outside. Sweat covered my whole body. I waited, aiming for the spot where I'd seen Jeffords' hat.

"Have they told you?"

Jeffords' voice came from several feet forward of the place where I had last seen him. I did not understand why he kept talking, but he probably hoped his words would have a psychological effect on me.

My finger toyed with the trigger of my rifle and I wondered if it wouldn't just be better to end this here and now.

Jeffords was a significant problem, it would be nice to have him out of my hair, I just did not know what those above him would think of the situation.

If I had known Roth was still alive, it might have been one thing, but I had to assume she had died in all of this too.

I could easily see them just not wanting to deal with it and ordering my death.

"Have they told me what?"

Jeffords laughed. "I knew you would. I knew you'd talk to me. You can't help yourself. You have to know. That's what drives you. You can't live with uncertainty." He laughed some more. "Your wife remarried. She had three more kids. Your son died in a tragic car accident. She even had plastic surgery and looks nothing like what you remember."

I didn't respond, but his words were having an effect on me. I doubted any of those things had happened, but I remembered Sam.

Sam.

The thought of him creeping on my wife at my funeral. Pretending to be a friend and the shoulder to cry on. Worming his way into—

Taking a deep breath, I sighted my rifle on the spot where I believed Jeffords to be and slowly started to depress the trigger, thinking that perhaps I had been misguided in my thoughts before and that I just needed to put an end to the man.

"We were saving that little gem. If you haven't figured it out by now, we like to keep our soldiers on their toes. That helps them do what we expect them to do. They obey orders better, especially after we break them." He chuckled. "That's what they ordered me to do to you. They wanted me to break you. To rip you down and build you again for our own purposes. I don't know how they managed to miss the fact that you and I had a prior history, the day you said your name it felt like I had just found the golden goose. The man I had been thinking about for twenty years while rotting in jail had been dropped in my lap on a silver platter.

"I thought about knifing you then and there, but I knew I was up next in the rotation and that I was going to be your drill sergeant. I knew that I could get to you. I knew that I could have my revenge and still have my life here too. That was one of the things I learned in prison. How to be careful." Jeffords laughed really long about that one and I almost pulled the trigger, surely if I sent three or four bullets his way, one of them would get through the canvas tent and whatever other obstacles might be in between us. It took every ounce of my resolve to keep my finger in place. He was trying to goad me. He was trying to make me angry. I knew all of this but his words had their intended effect. Not because of what he was saying, but because of this insane situation and the fact that he been trying to kill me ever since I had woken up here.

If I kill him, maybe I will finally have some measure of peace.

I shook my head and thought of Ava and Ricky.

They were why I could not do that.

I was still here because I had to know what happened to them. I had to do whatever I could to help them.

"I thought I had finally succeeded when you jumped into the ravine. Unfortunately, because they watch what I do, I had to make sure you at least had a chance to survive, so I gave you that. Barely. Somehow you managed to take advantage of it. It's better that it works out like this. I would much rather kill you myself than watch you die in an accident."

Twenty years. Did he say twenty years?

Had he really been in jail for twenty years?

It had not been that long yet at the time of my death.

None of it made any sense. Nothing he said added up.

"Your wife moved away from where they buried Ricky. She never even visits his grave."

"How long did you say you were in jail?"

Jeffords laughed. "I knew that would get you. I knew you'd latch onto that. I knew you'd wonder. If I'd been in jail for twenty years, how had it only been a couple since your death? It's a strange thing, time, a really strange thing indeed. There are some that believe time doesn't even exist."

I took a step forward. "Are you ready to do this? Let's just have it out, man-to-man. No weapons. Just you and me."

"What kind of fool do you take me for? There is no way I would do that. They made you the size of a great ape. I'd be foolish to try such a thing."

"Stand up and we'll finish this, enough of the chitchat. Enough of this talk. Let's just get this done."

"Because you can't handle the truth? Oh, Earl Anderson, there are so many more things I need to tell you. I want you to die knowing the full truth of everything. Your wife's next child was named Andy. Then she had a daughter named Sophie. And another son named Jeff. She never even told them about Ricky or you. It's just like neither of you ever existed. She has completely moved on and you are no longer even in her thoughts. Her husband, is nothing like you. At least not like you were back there. He's a big burly man who takes good care of her."

"You can dispense with the lies. I don't believe any of them."

"Don't you? You know that some of what I'm telling you has got to be true. You're smart. You know that this story of it only being a few years since your death doesn't add up. I had to get through twenty years of appeals before they could finally execute me. That's what you're thinking, isn't it? Your wife is now old and gray, living alone with her husband, thinking of her living kids and never thinking about the past she once had with you."

"Yeah, yeah, I get it. Come up and we'll finish this, just as you want."

"Not yet. You are trying to skip all the best parts."

There was a movement to the side of me and I turned, bringing my rifle over, thinking that Jeffords had somehow played a trick on me.

I nearly pulled the trigger when I saw that it was Roth.

She had a rifle aimed at me.

15

My heart was in my throat and for a moment I thought she was going to shoot me, but she hesitated. She didn't say a word. I had aimed my rifle at her. Perhaps it was just a precaution that she had done the same.

I held it off to the side, aiming towards Jeffords' general direction. Once I did, she pointed hers towards Jeffords as well.

She brought a finger to her lips. Then she made a rolling motion with her hand like she wanted me to keep asking Jeffords questions.

"What are the best parts?" I tried to make my voice sound as tight as possible, so he thought his efforts were succeeding. I could almost hear his grin when he answered.

"I can't get to that right away, now can I? No, what if I told you everything I just said was a lie? What if I told you your wife is still alive and that she's been mourning for you every day? Even made a little vigil that she put up in the alley where you were killed. That would be what you'd want to hear, isn't it? That's what you would expect. She and Ricky stop by once a week to leave flowers."

I glanced over at Roth while Jeffords spoke, but I could not tell by her facial expression whether any of this was true. She slid forward on her feet like a hunter sneaking up on a deer. Another couple steps and I figured she would have the drop on Jeffords.

"That is what I expected."

I tried to make my voice sound like I was choking up, like I was close to tears, because I wanted Jeffords to get on with it.

Roth was now five steps away from having a clear view of him.

"Well, that was true. It did happen. Like four years ago. Ricky is still alive, but he was in an accident and lost both his legs."

Roth took a final step. "The game's up, Jeffords. Drop your rifle."

I tightened my finger around the trigger, thinking that if Jeffords were about to make a rash move, I was in a solid position to take him out.

There was a long silence before Jeffords stood. He was several feet further along than I had predicted. He held his hands out.

"This is not what it looks like, General."

"I believe I heard you confess to attempted murder, is this not the case Sergeant Jeffords?"

"I was told to get Anders trained to go into the battle quickly, one of the components of my training is psychological."

"Did you order him to jump into a ravine before training him how to fly?"

Jeffords looked at me. "Ask him yourself but he'll probably lie because he hates me."

"I'm not playing this game with you, Jeffords. I'm tired of your insubordination. I'm tired of you needlessly sending soldiers to their death. And I'm disappointed to learn that you have used your position to seek vengeance. I know what you were before. Most of the rest of us might be killers, yes, but none of us are serial killers who killed just for the fun of it. I gave you the benefit of the doubt, hoping that a new body would mean a new man. It appears that was not the case." She motioned with a rifle. "Kneel."

"And why would I do that?"

"You are under arrest."

"You're not really going to do that."

"You're right. This is wartime. I don't have time for that."

Roth pulled the trigger.

16

Jeffords must have anticipated what she was going to do because he twisted when she pulled the trigger. He fell to the ground, probably in part because he had been hit by the bullet. I was already running around the side when Jeffords brought up his rifle.

"Shoot him, Anders," Roth screamed, as she fired again, right into his chest.

Jeffords fired, but it went high and only served to make Roth angrier.

I didn't pull the trigger.

I moved until I was right next to Jeffords' body, kicking the rifle out of his hands. I did not stop until it was a good ten feet away.

Roth approached while keeping her rifle trained on Jeffords, as if she expected him to get up and start moving despite the fact that his chest had been torn open.

Is she going to bring up my refusal to shoot him? I wondered.

"Check his pulse."

It was a strange order because there was no way he could still be alive, but I did as she asked and leaned down, touching his hand and felt nothing.

"He's gone."

"Let's hope he died fast enough." Once I was clear, Roth fired five more shots into him, including one into his head. There was no way he could have survived.

"I think you got them."

Roth fired one more. "Let's hope so."

I was taken aback by her strange actions, but did not comment. My goal was to get into her good graces and get off of this planet, not annoy her with a bunch of questions.

"Looks like Regina is going to have a mess on her hands."

"Excuse me?" I asked.

"Nevermind. Really good job out here soldier. Good work." Roth walked towards the south side of camp.

As I followed after I noticed the transport's engines still burned but with far less fuel than they had before Jeffords had started taking potshots at me. With one final look at Jeffords, just to convince myself that he was really gone, I followed after her.

I had hundreds of questions and wondered if it might be safe to ask a couple, but one look at her face told me that she was not in the mood to answer any of them. I followed in silence until we were twenty feet from camp.

Roth brought her watch to her mouth and pressed a button. "Open up."

I waited, expecting the sand in front of us to shift to reveal a secret underground garage, but nothing happened.

"This is General Katrina Roth. I am up on the surface, the lurkers have all gone and it's time for us to get out of here. Open up." She released the watch button. "It's bad enough those idiots tried to escape with the lurkers still on hand, don't tell me that all of them left too."

When nothing happened, I looked at Roth, expecting an explanation, but I did not get one.

"I have to do this myself. I am surrounded by idiots."

She walked until she was standing in the middle of the red sand. I thought she was going to do something again with her watch, but then she called out something that sounded like a specific keyword and a hologram appeared. She stepped up to it and pressed several translucent buttons.

A door opened in the ground, revealing an underground hanger.

17

A ladder allowed us to descend into the deep underground bay. After climbing down, we got to a concrete floor that was made with the ever-present red sand. A large crack ran down the middle of the hanger and the two remaining transports had been positioned so that they were on either side of it.

Was this crack made when the ravine opened up right after my arrival?

The hanger was spacious, far more spacious than I would have expected, considering the ground's instability. Even though there was much to look at, I kept returning to that crack in the middle of the floor, wanting to know how stable this place was.

At least I finally know why I didn't see any vehicles here. They were just underground. I was surprised there were no land-based vehicles, but maybe there was another hangar where they were kept.

This was kept hidden to keep recruits like me from wanting to run at the first opportunity.

The transport ships were similar to the one that was still burning up on the surface. If I listened, I could hear the roar even down here.

"If we had these all along, why didn't we use them against the grenlings?" I asked, the question slipping out before I had a chance to think better of it.

Roth looked at me and did not answer. She touched her ear.

"Anybody here?" Roth called out.

When she did not get a reply, she answered my question.

"These ships aren't armed with the type of weapons that we need to take out a grenling. The weapons they have are not very useful. Though after the events of the last few days, I expect that will change in the future." She shrugged. "Of course, it does not look like we're going to be on this planet much longer, so perhaps it's a moot point." She walked over to a bank of computers. "Now be quiet, I need to figure out what's going on."

I gave her a curious look. When had she tried to communicate with somebody else?

She touched her ear a moment ago.

That was what the soldier outside of Roth's office had done to create a protective bubble to communicate without being overheard. I assumed that Roth had done the same thing and that I had just not noticed.

I watched as she touched the computer screen and brought up a list of options, she moved so quick I did not have time to comprehend what she was doing. I was fascinated by the computer. When I took a step forward to get a better look, Roth looked over her shoulder and glared at me.

I stepped back and examined the underground bay instead. There was space for three transports and it looked like the only way out was to either climb up the ladder or take a transport.

Or use anti-grav boots.

I pressed the buttons on my watch, but they still did not engage. That was one thing I would talk to Roth about as soon as I thought she might listen.

A bank of computer screens drew my eye. I had taken several steps towards them but stopped when I saw what they were.

Security cameras.

The screens rotated through footage, coming from locations all over camp.

I had not seen a single camera up above.

I checked over my shoulder to make sure Roth was not looking at me, and then continued to watch as the screens rotated. There were not just dozens of cameras, there were hundreds, and all of them rotated every ten to fifteen seconds. There was at least half a dozen inside the brig.

Did somebody watch me get attacked by the crocks?

They did nothing.

I muttered a curse when I realized that somebody must also have seen the attack by that flying creature outside the ravine.

My hands clenched into fists.

When Roth had killed Jeffords, I had started to believe that perhaps my conspiracy fears were unfounded. But seeing this place, it set them stirring anew. It seemed like I was not so far off in some of my guesses after all.

They saw everything I had done at the brig, and did nothing. They saw everything I had done on the battlefield, and did nothing.

When Roth had called down here, she had expected people to be manning the station and had been surprised when they had abandoned their post. It was not much of a stretch to believe that during the entire battle with the grenlings, somebody had been sitting here monitoring the situation.

Perhaps, because this was a training environment, they were under orders to monitor but not intercede.

I shook my head, wondering who else had known about this place. Jeffords had known. He had told us to organize on the south side of camp, it had been his intention to get into the transport and leave. He had just waited until after he'd ordered me to do a lap.

He had wanted to save the others and let me die, but it had worked out in reverse.

It's funny how things sometimes happen, I am glad now that he ordered me to run a lap.

I checked on Roth again, hoping to have control of my anger by the time she realized what I had figured out, but she was still focused on the computer consul and had not given me a second glance after warning me to step back.

I turned back to the security cameras, wondering just how many of my actions had been caught by them.

In the battle with the grenlings, had the security guards been so focused on the battle that they had not paid attention to me? Or was there something to my concern that it had been a test?

Another thought occurred to me.

Jeffords' apparent disclosure of information about the camp which he had pretended to be against the rules had almost certainly been caught on camera too. If he had known about the transports, he would've known about the security guards watching these videos.

He had been playing with me, just as I had expected.

No big surprise there.

I let out a long breath and thought about how readily Roth had killed Jeffords, trying to calm my nerves.

In the end she had done what I had wanted to do but had not because I had been afraid of the consequences.

Another wave of relief flowed through me when I realized that if I had left Jeffords on the battlefield to fend for himself, they would have known about it.

I was glad again for the choice I had made.

It had been an instinct and the memory of my wife that had made me help Jeffords.

I had made my choice as if expecting somebody else to learn what I had done. That was something I had tried to do as an attorney and it appeared to be a good mindset here too.

Assume somebody is always watching because they probably are.

Even though that was a paranoid thought, it appeared well-founded for my present environment.

Knowing the level of monitoring that had been going on also helped me discard some of my wilder conspiracy theories.

This place was messed up, no doubt, but there had to be a rhyme and reason to the full organization; otherwise, it would fall apart.

Hopefully, my experience and situation were out of the ordinary.

Roth's unequivocal execution of Jeffords had given me some faith in the circumstances in which I now found myself. It also helped that I was slowly coming to terms with the fact that there was no way out of this.

I was stuck here.

I had to deal with the situation as I found it.

A faint hope still burned deep inside me that I would find my family. As much as I wanted to always keep them top of mind, my passion to find them had got in the way of making sure I kept a level head.

It was time for that to change.

Roth's words broke into my thoughts. "We have been attacked by two lurker carriers."

"What does that mean for us?" I asked.

"It means this planet is finished. The lurkers don't leave much behind."

She must have seen the look on my face as I imagined the entire planet being destroyed because she continued. "With time, the resources will all be consumed by the lurkers. Everybody is going to abandon this world by tomorrow or risk being caught."

"There is not a way to fight back?"

"Not with this many on hand. Our chief tactic—" she gave me an appraising look as if wondering if she were saying too much "—to this point has been guerrilla warfare. Most are not aware of what's going on in the day-to-day of the war."

"What happened to earth?"

Roth hesitated and then muttered something I didn't catch. "Earth was consumed a long time ago. It is now a vast wasteland." She held my gaze, unflinching and without blinking. I returned it even though I was starting to feel uncomfortable and could not help but remember how we'd had a similar exchange when we first met. In that meeting, I had been about to break the gaze when she had given in first.

"I know you found that old bible," she said at last. "I'm sorry you had to learn the truth about it that way, but it has been hundreds of years since earth was abandoned."

"Why the deception?"

"We have learned to introduce things slowly. We tried at first to let people know that they were now hundreds of years in the future but it did not go over well. The people who initially thought that just a few years had passed fared better."

"You lied out the gate."

"For good reason. Otherwise, we wouldn't have the stable system we have here."

"I have to believe if you would have told me the truth upon awaking—"

"You would have gone crazy just like everybody else." She gave me a searching look. "Do you mean to tell me that you have not thought earnestly about returning to your family this whole time? What if you had learned right upon awaking that they were dead, not just for a few years, but for centuries? That your whole life had passed you by and that everyone you ever knew was dead? That you had missed everything?" She shook her head. "How would you have responded? Trust me, we've been through this and have looked at this every which way. We hate the fact that we must engage in such deception, but so far, it's been the only way forward."

She came a step closer. "I'm sorry you had to find out the way you did, we generally introduce the topic a little bit better than somebody stumbling upon the truth, but to be frank, I don't have time to coddle you. I don't know if any of the lurkers are going to come back, their tactics and strategies at times appear quite erratic, so we have to get outta here if you're done playing twenty questions."

"Where do we go from here?"

"It is time for us to abandon the planet, I have reported in but haven't—"

She touched a finger to her ear and went silent, turning her back to me so I couldn't tell if she was speaking.

I was taken aback by her sudden willingness to answer questions, but at the same time, I was certain there was still vital information that she held back.

This is like an onion.

Every layer is going to bring something new.

18

To: Brigadier General Katrina Roth
From: Lieutenant General John Lincoln

Log date: 00429.211-10:49:13

Re: Package Request

General Roth,

I am not sure what you are talking about. Can you please provide me with further information?

Lieutenant General John Lincoln

19

Roth still had her back to me, so I wandered around the hangar, hoping to learn something useful. It was good to finally get some answers from Roth, but I now had more questions.

In the end, Roth had made it clear that she was done talking and even getting a little impatient.

My instincts told me that this information was what Jeffords had promised right as the invasion had commenced.

I had been further inducted into the organization by the disclosure of this information.

It must mean she trusts me now.

Or she just doesn't care anymore.

When I came to a row of rifles, I could not help but feel chagrined that others had been trained on them right away while my outfit had not.

Jeffords was to blame for that and he was no longer alive. I needed to let it go.

There was a bathroom, complete with a shower, and a small kitchen. Beside the kitchen was a bunk room with six cots. This appeared to be a self-contained living environment for the people monitoring the soldiers.

The hangar answered some of my questions about the camp, but not all.

I looked for more answers as I made my way around the hangar, trying to act nonchalant. Roth had made it clear that we were going to leave, but I expected to find similar setups in other worlds. I wanted to make the most of understanding this one while I could.

My eyes kept going back to the bank of security monitors from wherever I was in the hangar, the questions about what these people had been doing down here coming to mind again and again.

Had they known exactly what was going on with Jeffords the whole time?

More importantly, had Roth known?

Round and round the questions went. I initially tried to set them aside, hoping that one day I might find answers, because Roth was not likely to answer anything else today. She had already given me far more than I thought I was going to get and it was best to be happy with that for the moment.

My breath froze in my chest when I came around the side of a transport ship.

Another alien creature.

It was metallic and fierce looking. It had done nothing when I appeared. I stepped forward to get a better view inside the room where it was located.

It suddenly dawned on me what this was. I glanced over at Roth, but she was not looking my direction.

After another look at her, I went inside.

The room was filled with suits.

These were not the spacesuits I had become accustomed to thinking of when NASA sent people into space.

These were a class all their own.

They were meant for battle.

If they had one big enough for me, it would add to my already considerable stature. The suit itself was about eight feet tall. My eyes narrowed when I wondered if I *could* fit inside one. The next suit was a different size.

Do they make one big enough for me?

The suits were positioned so a soldier could get inside quickly.

If the suit had not been open, I might have gone back to Roth and reported we were not alone in the cavern. I was glad I had gone towards the source of my concern, rather than turning away from it.

In fact, that was a metaphor for this place.

It was the approach I needed.

Immediate assumptions about this world can get a guy killed.

They wanted people that learned for themselves, that did things without having to be told, that understood because they had learned the hard way.

I had not seen anybody training in these suits, so I figured that this was something that we were trained on later, probably after they were certain we were not going to go crazy.

"I see you found the suits."

I looked back at Roth. "When do I get trained on these?"

"Normally, it would not be for several months yet. Unfortunately for you, it is gonna start right now."

She paused.

"Suit up."

20

To: Lieutenant General John Lincoln
From: Brigadier General Katrina Roth
Log date: 00429.211-11:01:02

Re: Package Request

General Lincoln,

I am coming for it myself. Please make sure your men don't abandon Camp Myers until I have it.

Brigadier General Katrina Roth

P.S. It is vital to you, me, and all of humanity that I get that package.

21

I looked at her face, expecting a smile or at least a dark chuckle to tell me she was joking, but there was nothing there. The piece of equipment in front of me looked like it was far more sophisticated than I was capable of handling on the spur of the moment. While it was true the anti-grav boots had been easy enough to learn, I doubted that the suit would work as well as that.

"Excuse me?" The question slipped out before I had a chance to stop myself, and I inwardly admonished myself for showing hesitation.

"You and I have been ordered to go to Camp Myers."

"Why—" I cleared my throat. "What is our mission?"

Roth gave an approving nod as if she realized what I had done.

"That is classified and you should never speak about what we do today. Suffice it to say, I am going to need your help, and the only way you are going to survive is if you wear one of these."

I looked at the rows of suits and then back at her.

"Which should I use?"

I had been about to say that none of them looked like they would fit, but had thought better of it.

"The suit adjusts to fit the man, just like your hat."

I hesitated and she smiled without mirth.

"Today you learn by fire." She tilted her head to the side and gave me a weird look. "That is how you have been learning anyway, at least if I understand how Jeffords was training you."

This finally seemed like the right opportunity to ask a couple questions about Jeffords.

I opened my mouth but saw that Roth looked as if she expected such questions and did not want to entertain them right now.

I hesitated but only for a moment. She was not going to give me any more answers.

"I would not have it any other way," I said.

"Attaboy."

The moment of tension passed.

Roth walked over to the first suit and put her watch up to the base of the neck. The suit spat out a question.

"Authorization code?"

Roth rattled off a number that was so quick I could not memorize all of it. I did catch the first six digits, though, so I committed them to memory.

"Who requests access?"

"Kathryn Roth."

"Authorization granted."

Roth pointed into the middle. "Step inside."

I looked from the suit to Roth and then back to the suit again. It had been made for a man who was about five feet tall even though it was over eight feet itself.

I stepped up.

The suit adjusted and expanded until the space inside had grown so that it would fit me. The outer height and width of the suit expanded as well, making the suit more than nine feet tall. I tried to determine if the skin of the suit had stretched, but it looked the same to me.

I started to turn around, intending to step in backward, when Roth spoke up.

"Step into it, face forward."

"I thought that was the front," I said, pointing to the side I had seen when I had mistaken it for a monster.

"These suits look the same from the front or the back, it helps disorient the lurkers and makes them underestimate us." She growled. "I wouldn't rely on that if I were you, they are still just as lethal as a lion and as intelligent as any genius you have ever known. Most of us are dumb animals compared to them, even though they look like insect-mammal hybrids."

I removed my hat. "What do I do with this?"

"You can stuff it in between your side and the suit," Roth said, "it won't get in the way."

I did as instructed and stepped into the suit, perspiration forming on my face.

Back on earth I had sometimes been a little claustrophobic, and I felt that anxiety creeping up in the back of my mind. It was not nearly as bad as it had been back on earth, so perhaps being in a new body made it more palatable.

There were places where my skin connected directly with the suit: my face, neck, and hands. I had expected the metal to be cold, but it was warm to the touch. When I had inserted my hands, it had felt like I had slipped into a coat backward. My fingers touched buttons that were similar to a video game controller. I could also feel each of my individual fingers against one another, so I had not slipped them into a glove apparatus of some sort. Once my head was fully inside, something wrapped around my back and strapped me in, causing another wave of claustrophobia to run through me.

I swallowed and closed my eyes. There wasn't anything for me to see anyway, but it seemed to help.

"Tell your suit to wrap up, say it just like that," Roth said, her voice far away.

"Wrap up," I said, hating how uncertain I sounded.

I heard a quiet whirring as the suit closed around me, making me feel like I had just stepped into a coffin. I had a sudden intake of breath that I hoped Roth was unable to hear. When I opened my eyes it was dark, but then I could see again, like I was looking directly out of my eyes. I had expected a screen or goggles, but it was as if I was not in the suit.

I turned my head to see that Roth was getting into the suit right next to me, again this felt like a natural movement of my body and I did not even think about the fact I was wearing a suit.

When I spoke, I heard my voice plainly as if I still stood right beside Roth.

"What do I do next?" My voice did not sound as bad as it had a moment before, it helped that my eyes felt like they were viewing the world uninhibited by the suit.

"Take a step forward, be careful about it, it is going to take some getting used to, but it should be close to how you walk without it."

I did as instructed and found that it felt *exactly* like walking without the suit. She had made me so cautious that I expected I might stumble, but nothing like that happened.

I took another step and twisted around, feeling like it was just my own body and that I was not strapped into some gargantuan behemoth.

"Jeffords did actually train you on the antigravity boots, correct?"

"Yes, he did." I thought about bringing up the finer points of his training but decided against it.

I didn't want to say things had turned around, but they were going far better than they had been before.

"This suit acts in much the same way. It will respond to voice commands. I don't have time to teach all of them to you right now, but I will teach you a few things."

"Come with me." She took a step towards the door which I now realized was wider and taller than the other doors in the underground hangar. "By now, you understand that the suit moves naturally and feels like an exact extension of your body, but you must be very careful. Do not try to pick anything up. Try to avoid brushing up against or touching anything. I'm not going to try to teach you the intricacies of touch just yet, that is a skill that is hard to learn."

I followed Roth into the hangar, where she turned around and looked at me. Surprisingly, I could see her face through the visor of her suit.

"How well does this protect my head?" I asked.

"It's like you're wrapped inside a tank, so it does a good job."

"Your face is right there," I said, shaking my head and feeling the faintest sensation that the suit was moving with me.

"It is an optical illusion. In fact, everything you see right now is an optical illusion of sorts. You are not looking through your eyes, what you are experiencing as vision is a transmission that goes direct to your brain, skipping your eyes completely. The face that you see is only visible to another person in a suit. Somebody looking at me without a suit would not see anything but the suit. This has been engineered to help easily identify people while in combat, there are some other things as well that are similar, but we will get there as we go."

I was impressed with the suit. Other than the rehabilitator, I had thought that much of their technology was quite limited, but my assumption was wrong.

They kept it back because they wanted to make sure they could trust us.

My instincts told me that if we had not been attacked by the lurkers, I would not have been trained on the suit anytime soon, regardless of what Roth had said. It was only the present predicament that had prompted Roth to take the chance on me.

How is it transmitted directly into my brain? I wondered, while looking down at my hands and receiving a small shock when I only saw my suited arms. I had expected to see my hands because the experience felt so totally like I was in my body.

Even though my hands were free on the inside of the suit, I had appendages on the outside that represented the location of my hands.

I balled one hand into a fist and the suit did the same.

There was no lag, its response was instantaneous.

Weird but cool.

I could also see the suit around me. If I craned my head I could see down to my suited feet.

"Engaging the antigravity function of the suit is the same as using your boots," Roth said, "however, don't do it yet. Observe me first."

I watched as she reached over and touched two buttons on the arm of her suit in the same position where her watch was underneath.

Once she pressed the buttons she hovered in the air about a foot, I would've expected a visible propulsion force keeping her there, but it was exactly like how the anti-grav boots had worked.

Floating and silent.

"You have noticed by now, of course, that there are buttons right by your hands inside the suit, try not to touch any of them. If we have time, I will go into what they are for later. The antigravity buttons are an essential feature of your suit and require ease of use when under fire, so we put external buttons on the outside in the exact same position as a wristwatch. These buttons are two of only a handful of buttons that are available on the outside." She gracefully slid forward through the air like she was skating on ice and stopped when she was right in front of me. She reached out a hand and touched the same two buttons on my suit, but nothing happened. "The antigravity can only be activated by you. Somebody else cannot enable it; obviously, this is done for safety reasons.

I reached to activate my suit, but she put her hand out and stopped me.

"Wait!"

I was surprised by the biting response, it must have shown on my face because she went on. "Don't do it right here." She motioned towards a spot underneath the open door of the hangar. "Go over there before you engage."

I did as instructed and once I was in place, I turned to face her. She nodded and I engaged the buttons, immediately feeling myself lift off the floor. Even though my suit hands were not connected to my real hands, I felt pressure on the tips of my fingers where the suit's hand had touched the buttons.

"Unfortunately, despite all of the advances we have made in technology, one of the things that we have had a difficult time figuring out is how to make the suit respond in the exact same way as the anti-grav boots. I want you to gently push your toes down to the floor. I cannot emphasize this enough: it must be as gentle as you can possibly make it because you're going to—"

I didn't hear the rest. When I moved my toes, I shot up into the air and straight out of the hangar. Before I knew it, I was two hundred feet above the ground.

I swallowed and was glad I had come to a halt instead of continuing to shoot straight up. I looked down and saw that Roth was coming up to join me, moving far slower than I had. The seconds ticked by, it occurred to me that she was showing great control over the suit.

I had thought nothing of it when she had floated towards me on the floor before, but I now realized that it took significant skill.

Roth was soon beside me.

"You now understand how difficult it is to hold onto the suit. If I had let you engage the suit where you had stood, you would have buried yourself into the ground and I would've left without you."

That is not an idle threat, I thought, remembering how she had left me when the grenling had attacked the camp.

"I barely moved my toes." I shook my head. "I barely moved them."

"It takes practice to control your suit. I want you to gently spread your toes."

I did this, doing my best to hardly move at all and shot backward. A moment later Roth was right by my side. "Look behind you, carefully, without moving your feet."

Perspiration broke out on my forehead when I did as requested. If I would've gone another twenty feet, I would run into a cliff.

"The antigravity feature of the suit is extraordinarily sensitive. During my time here, they have tried different variations of the suit. None have been able to satisfactorily mimic the superior responsiveness of the anti-grav boots. In past versions of the suit's software, they adjusted the functionality so it did not respond nearly as well as the boots, but there was an outcry from the soldiers, and they found it was better if they just made it as sensitive as they could."

She floated until she was right in front of me. "When you get to battle you're going to be glad the suit is so responsive. I was one of the soldiers on the battlefront who threw up a ruckus when it was dumbed down."

"What's the secret?" I asked, believing that there had to be something more that I did not understand.

She shrugged, at least I thought that was what she did, it was hard to tell because the suit mimicked her, but only to a small degree. "There isn't one. You just have to practice. Now, I want you to spread your heels apart, do this as slow as possible and imagine that you're doing it before you actually do it and see what happens."

I slid forward thirty feet.

I could not recall moving my heels, but then I did the same thing again, focusing on thinking about it rather than doing it. I found that I had better control of the suit if I let my body subconsciously handle the movement.

I repeated the process, letting my instincts take over. It seemed to work far better, though not to the degree of control Roth had over her suit.

"I want you to land beside the hangar and watch me."

I flew until I was over the hangar, but then it occurred to me that I didn't really know how to go down. My use of the antigravity boots before had always been to go up. The only times I had landed, I had only been a foot off the ground, so it hadn't been a problem to simply disengage the anti-grav boots.

In another situation I might have experimented, but I didn't want to risk moving my feet and have something unexpected happen.

"General Roth, I don't know how to go down."

"What?"

"Jeffords never taught us." I thought about elaborating but decided against it. The man was gone. I needed to get over it.

"Spread your feet apart. If you go too far, you're just gonna fall like a rock."

I didn't move while I imagined myself falling to the ground like a meteor and getting stuck, or worse yet, flattened. I had never had a fear of heights, but I was starting to develop one. I spread my feet apart using the same technique I had before, thinking about it more than actually doing it. I began to fall like a rock dropping through the air.

I brought them together and shot back up, cursing as I went. I must have moved my toes when I made the adjustment. I flattened my feet and waited until I came to a halt before trying to spread my feet apart again. This time I still felt like I was falling but with less force than before. I didn't bring my feet together until I was almost twenty feet from the ground. When I did, I shot up, but only by about ten feet this time. After I caught my breath, I spread my feet apart.

Before I could react, I was on the ground, having created miniature craters around my feet. It was a rough landing, I hated that there were indentations for Roth to see.

I reached over and pushed the buttons, turning off the suit's antigravity feature. I took a step and was relieved to be back on solid ground again. I had not enjoyed learning to use the anti-grav boots and could say the same about the suit.

Death awaits at every turn.

I turned towards Roth, who had not moved while I had found my way down.

"Are you ready?" There was a note of impatience in her voice that was more pronounced than it had been before.

"Yes," I said.

She rotated while in midair so she was parallel with the ground and then shot forward like she had been fired from a gun, flying like Superman.

As she sped away, I became confident that she was moving faster than a bullet. There was even a small sonic boom as she flew over a chain of red cliffs, disappearing into the distance.

My heart thumped in my chest as I wondered if maybe she had left me. If she had, it could have been far worse. At least I had a means of transportation now, though I hardly knew how to use it.

She flew back at an even faster speed, halting in midair. One moment she had been rushing along, the next she had come to a standstill.

She rotated again and then lowered herself gently to the surface, coming down lazily like a leaf floating on a breeze.

"When can you teach me to do that?"

"Not today. I've spared as much time as I could now to bring you up to speed. I did that mostly to make sure it was working. We have to get on with our mission."

"Are we going to take the transport, or are we going to fly in our suits?"

Roth hesitated. "If you were a veteran, I would say fly, but I am not encouraged by how difficult it has been for you to use the antigravity of your suit. We'd also need fuel at some point. It's best we take the transport, I'll just have to fly close to the ground and be careful in our approach. We can take the suits with us in the transport. We will probably park once we're closer to the camp and know more about what's going on. Stay here."

She hopped into the underground hangar. I waited for a good five minutes before I heard the ship's engines engage.

This was my first good look at the transport as the other had been destroyed before I had a chance to study it, and I recognized it as similar to the ship that had picked me up that first day after I had suffered a terrible sunburn. It was much smaller.

It still bothered me that while the grenlings had been wreaking havoc on camp, the transports and suits had just been sitting here unutilized. The destroyed transport had killed a lurker, so the transports at least had a weapon. Roth said they didn't have any useful weapons—the dead lurker notwithstanding—perhaps the ships could have been put to use in some other way.

Roth landed the ship as gently as she had used her suit. Before long the back opened and she appeared without the suit.

She motioned for me to join her. "Go inside, be very careful to not touch or brush up against anything. Don't jump on the ramp or you might break it. Wait for me, I will help you get out."

She disappeared into the underground hangar as I approached the ramp, putting one foot on before lifting the other. It felt like aluminum foil compared to the suit. I was afraid it would crumble underneath me.

The designers of the transport must not have anticipated somebody my size wearing one of the suits, because my head barely cleared the top of the hold. There were poles along each side. Roth's suit was secured to the far pole on the right.

By the time I was fully inside the ship and looked back, the door to the hangar had closed and all I could see was the red ground, like it had never been there. It felt strange to finally get answers to some of the questions that had been dogging me, but I was not about to accept everything Roth had told me as true.

Roth jogged back into the ship and pointed at a metal pole that was opposite to the one where she had secured her suit. "Carefully walk towards that pole and position yourself in the same way I positioned the suit on the other side, just approach until you barely touch it. Go slow, this thing can crush a car as easily as you can a soda can."

I took small steps as I approached the pole. Once I was right up against it, I waited for further instructions.

Roth leaned against the wall. "Wrap your hands around the pole, it is reinforced and hard to damage, but I urge you to be careful about how you do this anyway. It is meant to hold the suit in place, not withstand the incredible force you can bring to bear with your hands."

I lifted one hand and wrapped it around the pole. Surprisingly, it felt like I had my actual hand around the pole. After I had done that, I did the same with the other. How did the suit make it feel like I was touching the pole?

"Now, repeat after me these words." She gave me a moment to get ready. "Engage the hand locking mechanisms."

I said this and felt something happen in the suit at the hands, but could not describe it as anything other than that, a feeling.

"Now say: 'Open the suit.'"

I said this and it opened up behind me.

I was about to get out, but she held up a hand. "Stop. There is one more thing you need to say. 'Disengage the brace.'"

After I said this last bit, the straps that had wrapped around my head and back, disconnected and slid up into holes like snakes.

"You are now free to get out."

I moved carefully from the suit. I took a step and nearly fell over.

"That first step after you get out is always a doozy, which is strange, because when you first get inside you feel like you're still in your own skin. It takes your body time to adjust to not wearing the suit, kind of like how it might feel after you went rollerblading or skiing back on earth. Give it a few minutes and everything will get back to normal."

22

I took my seat in the copilot's chair right next to Roth, nervous about going towards the lurkers instead of away from them.

Anything is better than training with Jeffords, I just wish it didn't mean I was heading into the fire.

"How far out is Camp Myers?" I asked.

"About five hundred miles."

"We could go that far in our suits?"

"Yep. They're basically mini spaceships. We would need to refuel. If Camp Myers is still there, that won't be a problem, but if it's not…" She left the thought unfinished.

"The suits run on fuel?"

"The propulsion system does, not the antigravity. That always works as long as there's juice." She flipped a switch. "Now be quiet, I have not flown a transport in years."

I shut up and tried to make sense of the dashboard in front of me. I had been in the cockpit of an airplane back on earth—never to fly it myself, but just with a friend who had a pilot's license—and this looked simpler than that. Roth and I both had dashboards in front of us that were identical. There were switches, levers, and buttons, but the main part of the console was taken up by a large touchscreen.

I watched as Roth used hers as easily as I might have a laptop computer back on earth, flipping so fast through various screens that I had no comprehension of what she was doing.

Roth touched her ear and was suddenly talking again in that silent, invisible bubble.

The conversation lasted for several minutes before she touched her ear again and turned to me. "The battle at Camp Myers has gone poorly. We must hurry if we are going to accomplish our mission."

"And what exactly was that?"

"It's classified. Don't ask again." She looked at me. "Seriously, don't."

I sighed and settled down in my seat as she engaged the ship's engines. We gently lifted into the air with her subtle touch. My experience with the suit had been exhilarating, but I preferred this method of travel. Roth kept low to the ground and headed in the same northwest direction I had seen the lurkers go.

A few minutes later, I recognized the mountain that Jeffords took us to climb and was glad that I was in a ship heading away from this place, even if it meant we were heading towards a battle with a classified mission.

Using gear that I've only trained on for a few minutes.

We made good time as the ground sped by underneath us. The consul touchscreen in front of me showed the same information as Roth's, and if my read of it was correct, we were going over six hundred kilometers an hour.

I was surprised at how easily Roth was able to navigate, considering how close we flew to the ground.

"The ship has shields," she said as if reading my mind when we got a little close to a hill, "not enough for us to withstand heavy fire, but enough that we can make haste today without being worried too much about stuff on the ground."

I cleared my throat and refused to make eye contact as I peeled my white-knuckled hands off the armrests and hoped that Roth had not noticed. I had never been exactly comfortable on airplanes back on earth and this was a more intense experience than that. The ground sped by at an alarming rate, and Roth was so casual about the way she flew, that I was concerned we might run into a mountain before she knew what she was doing.

"I don't see much vegetation here," I said to get my mind off of things, "is that true of the whole planet?"

"We are in a desert. There is vegetation, it's just in unlikely places."

"Like down a ravine?"

"Exactly. There are gigantic rain forests on this planet, perhaps one day you might return and see them because they are worth the trip, it makes the redwoods look like something children made. The trees are thousands of feet tall and hundreds of feet in diameter. Our scientists believe them to be tens of thousands of years old."

I wanted to know more, but I had another important question on my mind.

"Are the grenlings sentient?"

"Who knows? I have wondered myself. When we originally took control of this planet, we believed it to be uninhabited and mostly barren. The rain forests are the exception rather than the rule, most of this planet is covered with desert. There are a few seas, but they are small. So are the lakes, they all look like ponds next to the Great Lakes. There is nothing even approaching a network of oceans. The grenlings live in ravines and usually come out at night. It wasn't until after we had already taken up residence that we realized they were here."

"They wear armor."

"That is a mystery nobody has solved. We have never seen them make it—nobody's ever really payed much attention to them—but it would appear that they are more intelligent than we give them credit for."

"How many are there?"

"I have no idea."

"Are there any other sentient races here?"

"Not that we've found."

I settled back and avoided asking any more questions because we were heading towards a mountain range, I wanted to make sure she was focused on navigating through it.

When we were a mile out and she still had not turned to the left or right, I knew she intended to go through.

She looked over at me. "Buckle up."

After I put on the seatbelt, I also grabbed onto the sides of the chair.

The mountains came quick and soon loomed in front of us, and for the first time I saw vegetation out in the open rather than just down the ravine.

At first it looked like the lower part of the mountains were covered with trees similar to what I might find back on earth, but as we got closer, I recognized they were different. We moved too fast for me to discern the particular details, but the structure appeared intricate.

"Jeffords told me that summer is much hotter, is that true?" I asked, forgetting my resolve to not ask questions while she dealt with the mountain range.

"Yeah, enough questions. Hold on, this is gonna get dicey, time to put it on autopilot."

I nearly swallowed my tongue and tried not to think about what we were doing as we headed straight into the mountain range without slowing in the slightest.

Mountains zoomed by on either side. Roth grabbed her armrests, letting the ship's autopilot do all the hard work.

I was glad to know we weren't relying on her reflexes, but I wasn't sure that I had much more confidence in the ship's computer. Even though they had remarkable technology, I had not yet seen the ship's navigational capabilities and I was getting a first-hand look at what they could do while my life was on the line.

We zoomed by a rockface that looked like it was no more than a foot away. The slightest error would send us careening to our deaths. The ship continued at the same speed as if it was nothing.

It adjusted, moving closer to the rockface.

Roth's brow furrowed.

"What are you concentrating on?" I asked.

"Quiet. I'm trying to keep my stomach from upheaving."

I was surprised by her blunt honesty, especially since she had gone to such a great effort to cultivate an image that was at odds with showing weakness. She looked just as pale as I felt.

I shook my head and kept my eyes forward, hoping we would soon be through the mountain range so we could relax.

Relax?

We're headed into battle.

The ship shifted every moment, turning slightly to the right or the left, at one point, we had a steep climb. I could have sworn that we flew up a cliff with just inches to spare between us and the rockface and then just like a roller coaster that hit the top of an arch, we crested and went back down the other side.

"We normally don't use it like this!" Roth's voice was high-pitched, and while I would not have called it a scream, it was something close.

I shook my head and felt bile rising in the back of my throat, which I somehow managed to swallow. I closed my eyes for a moment of respite before opening them again in time to see us hurtling towards another cliff, this one taller than the last one we had gone over like a roller coaster. At the last moment, we banked hard to the right, and I could've sworn I felt the bottom of the shuttle dragging on the mountain. I thought of the shields Roth had mentioned and shook my head, hoping we'd somehow make it out of this alive.

The twists and turns lasted for several long minutes after that, but it seemed like we were through the worst.

I sighed in relief when I saw a clear path up ahead.

It was not long before we were out. I resumed normal breathing, starting with several deep breaths to get the oxygen flowing.

The ship leveled out and resumed its course as I looked over at Roth to see her unclenching her hands from her seat. She moved them to the console and typed something in.

"I'm sending us down to fifty feet."

"How does this thing avoid obstacles? Like trees and small hills?"

"Small trees aren't a problem, we just go right through."

I looked over and saw she was serious. "How many times have you done this?"

"This is the first."

"Seems you know what to expect."

"We were heading towards a mountain range, and I had told the ship to stay below two hundred feet, kinda saw it coming."

I looked back over my shoulder, expecting to see the mountains behind us, but, of course, I just saw the hold of the transport ship. The suits had remained in place, not even moving an inch out of place or twisting to either side.

There were several brief moments while we both reoriented, she seemed as lost in her thoughts as I was in mine.

"We have another one of those coming up?"

"We have some small hills, but nothing like that. It should be relatively smooth sailing from here until right before we get there."

"Famous last words."

Roth grunted. "Indeed, considering where we are going."

Before we had gone into the mountains, I had a list of questions I wanted to ask Roth, now all of them were gone. There was only one question in my mind now. The question that had been there since I had arrived.

Where is my family?

I considered asking, but my instincts told me I needed to shy away from it, at least for now.

Asking if she had ever connected up with anybody from her former life was probably just as taboo as talking about before.

"One of the things I neglected to go over when we were using the suits was how to use the weapons." Roth looked over at me. "I did this on purpose. You should focus on surviving, rather than fighting. Our mission should be relatively quick, don't ask what we're doing," she said, apparently noticing the look on my face, "it *is* classified. The suit will help you survive while you provide me with support. It will give you the means and the ability to fight a lurker in hand-to-hand combat, so I'm not gonna give you access to the weapons just yet. The suit's shield should be adequate. It will keep most of the lurker's weapons at bay. If a ship hits you, you're dead, of course, so look out for those."

"Why not show me how to use the weapons? If things are as bad as you say, it seems like you will need all the help you can get."

"Yes, but I don't want you making mistakes and killing innocent lives or destroying things that are better left untouched." She turned and gave me a severe look. "I want you to focus on one thing, surviving. Not fighting."

"This is just like what Jeffords did to me with the boots." This was something I never would've said to Jeffords, and even though I was challenging her authority in a way, Roth did not take it as such. She appeared a little more open to suggestion than Jeffords had been, so it was a calculated risk on my part to bring it up.

"Yes, I remember you mentioning that, didn't you say he somehow deactivated your boots?"

"They would only work at certain times."

"I've never heard of that before," Roth said to herself as if she were thinking of something else, she opened her mouth as if she was gonna say something but then apparently thought better of it and shut it again.

"Are you telling me that what Jeffords did was not officially part of the sanctioned training program? He made it seem as if he did it all the time."

"Perhaps he did, but it never got back to me. I'm telling you I've never heard of anybody doing that before. Maybe it was all just in your head."

"I watched him bring up a holographic display on his watch and disable our boots." I gave her a searching look. "I did not almost die in the ravine solely because I didn't know how to activate the boots." I thought about explaining how Jeffords had left me to figure that out on my own, but I was dealing with enough at the moment. "It was because he disabled the boots, and he didn't enable them until I was nearly at the bottom, apparently thinking I would die."

"Amazing." Roth shook her head. "Just simply amazing. I don't know how he managed to do it. I frankly have no idea. It's amazing you survived at all."

"I can't tell you how many different times I tried to get my anti-grav boots to work during the battle with the grenlings, but they never did. They should've worked, right?"

"They should have."

"Is there a way to figure it out?"

"The man is dead. I put him into the ground myself. I think you need to get past this."

I couldn't resist. "Was it a part of the training program to have us jump into the ravine without teaching us first how to use the anti-grav boots?"

Roth arched an eyebrow as she hesitated. "No, that is not how the training is supposed to happen." She glanced over at me. "But to be honest, it's probably a good thing he did do that to you. If I had not heard about what Jeffords had done and how you had responded, I might have just left you back there in camp to fend for yourself, instead of thinking you might be useful to me on our mission."

I was taken aback by this comment and didn't quite know how to respond, so I sat in silence.

Eventually, Roth looked over. "Jeffords was hard on you, no question. He did things he shouldn't have done. I heard about how he sent you to the brig, accusing you of killing a man. There was a full autopsy done, it was completed just before the grenlings attacked. That recruit died of natural causes.

"A heart attack, in fact. If I were to venture a guess, I would say it was most likely brought on by the fact Jeffords was doing things like having you guys jump into ravines without teaching you how to use your anti-grav boots."

She paused as if thinking carefully about what she was going to say next. "But you should be grateful for the training Jeffords sent you through. It woke you up to the truth about this world, this universe. This is not a peaceful place like earth. We are in a violent environment where you could die as easily walking down the street."

I did my best to keep my face from showing the cauldron of emotions that boiled underneath me, and perhaps I succeeded because Roth didn't say anything more about that.

On the one hand, I could see what she was saying about how Jeffords' unorthodox way of training had been beneficial, forcing me to learn things in a way that was different than was expected from the other new recruits.

But on the other hand…

I forced it all away.

I must remain focused on finding my family. Even if that means I leave some questions unanswered in the wake of Jeffords' death.

I thought of one more, and despite my resolve to leave the matter alone, I found that I could not shake this one. I had to know the truth.

"Did you know that Jeffords was a serial killer back on earth?"

Roth shot me a smile. "Who wasn't?"

I stared at her in stunned silence.

"Oh, come on, I'm joking. Yes, we knew he had that certain proclivity, but there has been research done to show that the makeup of the brain had a lot to do with that activity. We made sure that Jeffords didn't have the same type of brain he had back on earth."

"In other words, you improved him. You improved a serial killer."

"I guess you could put it like that if you wanted, but I think you need to ask yourself some hard questions about why Jeffords' had the tendencies he had back on earth."

"And all that research is mitigated by the fact that you had to put him down like a dog, right?"

"I'm not saying that it is or isn't. That's above my pay grade and frankly, my experience. All I'm saying is we have the technology to understand things about the brain that we did not over there. Do we know everything? No. Do we know a lot more? Yes. One of those things was understanding some of what made Jeffords a serial killer, not everything. For every man like Jeffords, there are others we gave second chances to who have turned out to be exemplary soldiers. She gave me a long glance. "Not because they were proficient killers, but because they were decent people who had lost the genetic lottery back on earth."

I wasn't convinced.

"And so you change their brains, hoping to capitalize on the good parts while negating the bad."

I said this last bit as carefully and unemotionally as I could, but my tone must have shone through because Roth gave me a roguish smile.

"I know you were a lawyer. I mean, come on, can't one cutthroat cut another cutthroat some slack?"

She smiled to show she was joking, and I smiled back to show that I got it, but deep inside, I did not like this at all. I was relieved to learn that some of what Jeffords had done was not sanctioned by the overall organization. I also could not blame Roth for being pragmatic and taking advantage of what Jeffords had done to further her own needs.

On the other hand, it was as I feared. They *were* using serial killers by changing their brains, hoping to capitalize on their other "good" qualities.

That did not bode well.

23

Roth and I traveled in silence for the next several hundred kilometers, moving fast while only fifty feet above the ground. I was glad that Roth had opted for us to take the transport rather than come all this way in our suits because I was sure she would've left me behind by now. The nausea had subsided. I resolved not to let anything like that happen to me again. It was strange, but I was starting to actually look forward to seeing Camp Myers, even though it was going to be in the middle of a combat zone when we arrived.

Anything is better than training with Jeffords.

It also helped that I was finally making some progress in this insane place. Within the last couple of hours, I had met the creatures that were on the brink of destroying mankind and had been trained on how to use a military fighting spacesuit. Things were looking up, even though I could easily die within the hour.

What's new about that?

That's how it has been since I arrived.

Jeffords had told us that the desert went for miles and miles, clearly hoping to discourage us from trying to escape. We had gone almost three hundred kilometers without seeing anything other than more redrock and ravines, so I was inclined to believe that he had told me the truth about that. The ravines were everywhere. At one point, I thought I even saw a grenling in the distance, but by the time I realized what I was looking at and tried to focus on it, we had already passed, so I could not tell for sure.

I had not asked Roth any more questions and she had not volunteered additional information. What she'd already told me was enough to chew on for now. In our training, they had led me to believe that at some point we would be asked to give an oath to the organization we had been conscripted for. I was glad Roth had not yet tried to administer that.

I did not think I was ready for that.

I had pushed a little further than I probably should have with my questions, and it was time to change my approach because I wanted her to think that I was going to be a team player.

I finally broke the silence when we were a hundred kilometers out from Camp Myers.

"What is our plan when we get there?"

"Observe conditions on the ground and in the air, after we have a read of the situation, we're going to insert into Camp Myers. There is an object hidden in an underground location that was inadvertently left when the evacuation was ordered."

Who ordered the evacuation? I almost asked the question but decided I had far more pressing concerns.

"Aren't there still soldiers fighting the lurkers? I can't imagine we just evacuated without a fight. Why can't they complete the mission?" I was careful to use the word 'we' so it sounded like I was starting to assimilate to the group identity.

"Yes, there are still soldiers fighting, and no, they can't procure the item because it is highly classified. It's not supposed to exist. Rumors about this got around several years ago, we can't afford to let something like that happen again." Roth looked as if she had said too much, her mouth formed a thin line, and I could tell she was thinking of telling me to forget about that last bit, but then she shook her head and remained silent, perhaps not wanting to call attention to what she had said. I filed that information away for later use, hoping that I might figure out what she was talking about.

"It's so important that they're sending a general to fetch it."

It looked like it was painful for Roth to answer.

"Yes."

"Wasn't there a general on-site already?"

"You ask a lot of questions, you know that?"

"You implied that you like that I am a lawyer. That's what I'm doing. Investigating."

"Yes, there are usually at least two high-ranking generals at Camp Myers at all times. Only one of which has been read in on the situation, and she is out of the system. The other general has stepped in to manage the evacuation." Roth turned to me. "I know I'm asking for your discretion here, and you probably don't feel like

I deserve it, but I chose to bring you along because I believed you would be an asset. Don't make me think otherwise."

"I won't."

"Just think of me as a client from back on earth and we'll be fine."

A client?

I didn't think of her like that at all, I considered her my captor, but that was best not said.

"Enemy alert," a disembodied voice said, the message came from the consul, there were flashing lights on the screens. I watched as Roth turned her attention to the alert, her fingers moving quickly as she tried to figure out what was going on.

I scanned the horizon and did not see anything. We had a limited view of what was to either side of the craft and no view of what was behind us.

"It looks like a downed lurker ship," Roth muttered, she then let out a curse. "Several of our ships are beside it, looks like they've all been destroyed. I'm not picking up any survivors."

"Where?"

"That way." She pointed off to the left. I couldn't see anything, but several moments later, I saw a shape growing in the distance.

It also looked like insects were in the air hovering above it.

"Crap. They spotted us. They're coming our way." Roth was up from her seat and heading back to the hold. "Stay where you are."

I unbuckled my seatbelt and went after her, catching up to her while she got into the suit.

"I told you to stay put."

"I'm coming with you."

She grabbed me by the shirt and pushed me back into the wall. "No. You aren't. That was one thing Jeffords said about you that I believe. You have a hard time obeying orders. This can sometimes be seen as a virtue, and I understand you realize that too, but you have to lay off. There's a time to question and a time to just obey. This is one of the times to obey. You are not equipped for this, and you will die if you do try to follow. Your best shot is to stay on the ship. I will be right back."

I went over to my suit, intending to get in regardless of what she said.

Roth spat out a number and said, "Disable suit."

It closed before I could even get a foot inside.

Roth was already inside of hers and had released her hold on the pole. "When I get back, we're going to have a conversation about what it means to obey. I am going to cut you some slack, but not much. Keep that in mind."

She walked to the end of the hold, the ship shifting as she moved.

"You're going to want to hold on to something."

I grabbed a pole as the hold door opened.

Roth jumped out without another word.

24

To: Brigadier General Katrina Roth
From: Lieutenant General John Lincoln

Log date: 00429.211-12:24:13

Re: Package Request

General Roth,

I don't take kindly to your tone, but I will excuse it for now until you can explain your insubordinate attitude. The Camp Myers evacuation is underway, but I have already ordered my soldiers to leave behind as many lurker casualties as possible.

I previously told them to take an hour or two, I will extend that to no more than four hours.

Good luck.

Lieutenant General John Lincoln

25

I sat in stunned silence while I stared at the shut door, anger flooding through me. It took me a couple of moments to gather control before I returned back to my place at the front of the ship.

During the short time it had taken for her to suit up and go, we had already gotten close enough to the lurkers that the downed ships were identifiable. Not only that, no fewer than five of the creatures were now headed our way. They didn't look like insects any longer. I buckled into the seatbelt and estimated we had less than a minute before we converged.

"The ship's programed for evasive maneuvers," Roth said, her face appearing on the screen in front of me. "You stay put, and you'll be just fine."

I hesitated for a moment, but then realized I had only one response.

"Yes, sir."

"And one more thing, the evasive maneuvers are sometimes erratic. You're going to want to make sure you hold on tight, even if you're strapped in."

Her face disappeared, and I watched as she pulled up beside me, flying like she had before in a prone position, trailing a jetstream behind her like she was a miniature fighter.

I cinched my seatbelt up as tight as I could, pulling on both the chest and lap straps.

"Incoming enemy," said the ship's computer.

"How far out are they?"

There was no response.

"Not only am I trusting that the autopilot is going keep me safe, I have no way of communicating with it."

I shook my head as I reached out and touched the screen in front of me. It lit up, and I was immediately shown a display of the incoming lurkers. The lurkers were represented by little icons that looked like dragonflies.

When I looked over to my left at where Roth had been, it was just in time to see her shoot forward.

A dogfight in a flying suit with a lurker.

I was starting to think she might regret not training me on the ship's weapons when a burst of light came from her, tearing through one of the oncoming lurkers, sending two severed pieces flying in opposite directions. The lurkers fired their weapons at her, but she was already past them. She twisted in midair and looped back around, fired again and missed, the bolt going harmlessly into the ground below. As graceful as her move had been, the lurkers were faster and more agile. One had even appeared to stop right in midair before turning to go right back after her.

She's fighting creatures that have grown up flying.

I had thought she had a pretty good shot of surviving this, but seeing the lurkers in action made me think twice.

She had drawn three of the remaining lurkers, but one still headed in my direction. The ship made no movement during the exchange other than to continue forward. I glanced at the screen, the dead lurker was no longer represented on the radar.

When I looked back up, the lurker coming my way was now firing on me, using the same weapons I had seen earlier during the destruction of our camp. Several of the shots hit the ship, but they seem to be absorbed into the shields because I did not feel them and the ship was not harmed.

At least, if the ship gets damaged, I expect it will bring it to my attention.

"Engaging evasive maneuvers." The ship's computer had no emotion, but its words were accompanied by a high-pitched siren that made my blood rush all the faster through my body.

The ship climbed with enough force that it pushed me back into the chair like I had been shoved.

I had one final glance at Roth as she fired another shot and missed, before all I could see was the purple sky. The ship accelerated so fast that I felt like it was trying to weld me into the seat.

The ship suddenly stopped—sending me forward into my restraints with an oomph—and it began to fall as if the engines had just seized up. A moment later, I was looking down at the ground when it became clear that the ship was still in control because the engine engaged and we shot forward.

The evasive maneuvers were worse than Roth had described.

I reached for a nearby vomit bag that was attached to the wall but did not put it up to my mouth. I was determined to keep from throwing up, I had only reached out for it as a last resort. The last thing I wanted was for Roth to get back into the transport ship and laugh at me because there was vomit all over the place, it would only be slightly less bad if I threw up into the bag.

I saw Roth.

It appeared she had been swarmed by the lurkers and was about to go down, but then she sped straight into the air like a rocket, and while they chased after her, it was clear she had the advantage of speed, if not maneuverability. She took down another lurker. The remaining two followed her like dogs hunting a rabbit.

I caught one last glimpse of the lurker that was firing at me before the ship suddenly shot up in the air again. The contents of my stomach threatened to excavate themselves, but somehow I managed to swallow them back when I realized we were not accelerating as fast as we had before.

The realization helped me take control.

I figured the ship was in a curve because it started to slope downward. It leveled out and shot to the right.

I groaned. "The ship will kill me if the lurkers don't!"

The transport readjusted until it was back on course.

Roth just had one left. She sped away from the ship while that lurker followed.

A sudden weight landed on top of the ship.

Two lurker legs dangled down in front of the windshield.

26

I grabbed hold of the armrests expecting that the ship would respond by taking another evasive maneuver, but it remained in place as if it was paralyzed by the lurker. One second passed, then two. I counted off the seconds, hoping to shortly be delivered from the situation.

Soon it was ten seconds, and I found myself missing the wild maneuvers from before.

And then it was thirty seconds.

Perspiration dripped down my body as I frantically touched the screen in front of me, trying to figure out anything I could do. The only thing I could bring up was the radar screen that showed the lurker was right on top of me. I tried other options on the screen, but nothing happened. I looked desperately at the switches but didn't dare press one of those until I knew exactly what it would do. I studied the switch labels, but nothing stood out to me as an option that would remove the lurker from the roof.

As a last resort, I might try pressing some of them randomly, but I was not there yet. The ship did not appear to be in any immediate danger, or if the lurker was doing something, it wasn't obvious to me, so I would wait it out for as long as I could.

I was on the verge of unstrapping from the seat and trying to get into my suit—if the lurker brought down the ship, I would have some chance of surviving—when I remembered that Roth had locked it.

I cursed myself for having been belligerent enough to make her feel like she needed to leave it locked up.

The lurker's legs were still visible through the windshield.

I just had to hope that the shield held.

I focused my attention on the radar screen, trying to figure out what was going on with Roth. I saw an icon on the screen that I believed represented where she was, but it was so far away that it was almost off the screen.

The radar refreshed, she was gone.

Fearing the worst, I unstrapped from my seat and walked back to the suit.

She had rattled the number off twice, once before when she had activated it and once afterward to deactivate it. I examined the suit itself, thinking in vain that the number might actually be written on the suit, but I had no such luck.

I tried to remember the number. I could've sworn it was ten digits, I could still remember the six I had memorized. I placed my watch at the neck, said those, and then tried saying the next four numbers that came to mind, but nothing happened.

I went to the front of the ship to make sure the lurker was still there. It had not moved. I didn't know how it was disabling the ship, but I was getting desperate enough to try flipping one of the switches.

Last resort only, I thought.

Cursing, I went back to the suit and tried saying another number but had the same result.

I pressed the anti-grav buttons on my watch, half hoping that I might levitate, but that, of course, didn't work either. Whatever Jeffords had done was still in place.

He's gonna kill me from beyond the grave.

It was quiet at first, but it slowly came forward to my consciousness the louder it got.

A shudder went down my spine when I finally realized the noise was a saw cutting into the top of the ship.

27

Sparks fell through when the lurker's blade breached the ceiling. I cursed as I stood in front of the suit and said the words "activate suit" and tried a bunch of numbers, but nothing happened.

After no fewer than ten more tries, I looked at my watch display and flipped through a variety of screens, but didn't understand what half of them were. Roth had used her watch to communicate, but the feature was not apparent to me, so I could not call her. I tried the anti-grav buttons again, wishing I could just jump out of the hold and fly to the ground, but, of course, nothing happened.

Jeffords!

I let out a ragged breath and reminded myself that he was dead now and would never bother me again.

I went to the front of the ship and checked the radar display, hoping to see Roth squawking at me from the screen, but the only thing there was the radar with the lurker right in the middle.

The ship had not slowed in the slightest while the lurker had been trying to gain access.

"Engage evasive maneuvers," I said aloud.

The ship did not respond. I tried accessing more information through the screen again, but nothing seemed to work. The only thing I could see was the radar display.

I shook my head, looking around the ship for anything I might use a weapon but found nothing.

More sparks came through the hole now, and I could see more of the blade. I didn't know how long I had but figured it was minutes, if not seconds.

Cursing, I went back to the suit and tried finding the other outside buttons Roth had referred to, but nothing jumped out at me.

A large shower of sparks came through the opening. The full saw blade was now visible, it was as big as a dinner plate. There was a brief pause as the lurker lifted up the blade. I could see its eyes looking down through the crack it had made. I feared it would fire a weapon through the tiny slit, but it reinserted the blade and moved to widen the cut.

My blood rushed through my veins as I considered my options, thinking that the time was short before it had cut a hole big enough to shoot at me.

Going back to the consul screen, I tried to flip through it, hoping to find manual controls but could only bring up the radar screen. I tried Roth's monitor but to the same effect. I regretted my belligerence. I could easily have slipped into the suit and hopped out of the transport by now.

I checked on the slit.

It was now a foot long. At some point, it would cut another slit, but it was still working on the primary one.

I wasn't ready to follow Jeffords into the afterlife, not yet.

Not by a longshot.

There has to be a way out of this.

I returned to my seat and strapped in, closing my eyes and taking a deep breath. As I did, thoughts of the alleyway where I died flooded through my mind. I had thought that day I had the situation well in hand, but reality had slapped me upside the head and told me I hadn't.

This will not be like that. Not today.

Things were supposed to be easier once I no longer had somebody gunning for my death.

Lurker, Jeffords, or Sam, it's all the same. Too many people want me dead, and I'm determined not to go.

I took a deep breath and let it out slowly, remembering the first time I had witnessed Roth activate one of the suits. The numbers I didn't know seemed to be right on the tip of my tongue, but then they disappeared. I took another deep breath and tried to mentally return to that moment in time.

I had just found the suits.

Roth had walked in after finishing her call.

It was there, but out of reach, I shook my head.

I sat down in front of the suit, closed my eyes, and took another deep breath, trying to ignore the sparks that were raining down several feet away. There was a brief lull, but I did not look up.

A moment later, the rest of the numbers came to me.

I spat them out after touching my watch to the neck. "Activate suit."

The suit opened up. I looked on and was glad that nobody was around to see my dumbfounded face.

I was surprised it had worked.

When I stood, I noticed the lurker was now working on another slit. The saw had completely disappeared, but I could still hear it as it cut down into the ship. Every now and again, a spark would make it through the already formed slit and hit the floor.

It had taken a couple minutes for the lurker to breach the hold, so I figured that I had at least a couple more before it would cut through in a new place.

I hoped to hop off, just as I had seen Roth do.

"Authorization code?"

I said the same code I had used before and held my breath.

"Who requests access?"

A flood of relief flowed through me, but it was short-lived because I realized that Roth had used her name to gain access to the suit, I thought about just giving the suit her name but figured it was voice-activated.

"Earl Anders."

My name is Earl Anderson.

The suit did not respond right away.

Just as I was about to try putting my watch up to the base of its neck, it spoke.

"Authorization granted."

Taking a deep breath, I stepped into the suit, feeling the straps behind my head slither out like snakes and fasten in.

"Close the suit."

The suit didn't move. I frantically searched my memory for the exact words Roth had said.

"Shut the suit."

Nothing happened.

I had not come this far to fail now.

It took me a moment to remember, during which I checked on the lurker's progress. The saw was already through.

Wrap up.

"Wrap up!"

The suit closed around me, and the display sprang to life in my mind. I cautiously loosened one hand from the pole and then the other, afraid that the ship might lurch and cause me to lose my balance.

Just like before, moving was as easy as walking in my own body. I experienced a slight sense of disorientation because it felt like I had grown and become a metallic beast.

I also felt better about being inside the suit while standing in the hold, waiting for the lurker to cut in.

The lurker had almost completed the second slit, it had not taken nearly as long as I had anticipated.

I carefully took a step forward, remembering how Roth had caused the ship to sway when she moved. I didn't know how much the lurkers knew about our suits, but I didn't want the lurker suspecting that I had suited up.

I took another step and felt the ship lurch, whether it was because of me or something the lurker had done, I could not tell. Carefully, I shuffled to the back of the ship, making sure to skirt the slits, so the lurker did not know that the game had changed. The saw was just about to connect with the first slit when I got to the door. I looked at the button Roth had used to open it, took a deep breath, and then pressed it.

28

The door opened and the wind rushed all around me, but I did not fear that I was about to be sucked out as I had before because it felt like my feet were glued to the floor. Surprised, I took a moment to get my bearing. The desert sped by, but it looked just as flat as it had been for most of the way. There was a large hill off to the right, but it was easily avoidable. I waited for several seconds, figuring that the lurker would recognize what I had done and come to investigate.

If it did, I expected the ship would resume its evasive maneuvers, and I could close the door. I would escape without having to jump out.

The lurker made no move to release the ship, even though I was confident the drag had changed.

It would soon realize something was up.

It removed its saw from the second slit. I turned my attention to the door, expecting at any moment to see the lurker. I prepared to hit the button to shut it.

The lurker started cutting a third slit.

I snorted. *The door is open, you no longer need to cut your way in.*

If the lurker didn't soon realize what I had done, I had no other choice but to bailout. That was not a bad option, especially if I escaped without the lurker noticing until it was too late.

We were still fifty feet above the ground, zooming along past all sorts of obstacles. Another hill went by underneath, and I was glad I had not chosen that moment to jump out because I would have smashed into it.

It had come within several feet of the ship.

The top of the hill looked like it had been cut by something. Was that the work of the ship's shield? I glanced back through the front of the windshield and could just make out that we were heading towards another mountain range.

It's now or never.

I took a deep breath and jumped while pressing the anti-grav buttons on my suit. I fell, but only for a moment before the anti-gravs kicked in and had me hovering in the air. Pushing slightly down with my toes, thinking it more than doing it, I stabilized my position and turned to see that the ship was already several hundred feet away.

I thought I had escaped until the lurker detached and flew my way.

I stifled a curse. "Roth, are you there?"

There was no response.

I spread my toes apart and sped backward on instinct more than a conscious choice because the lurker was coming fast. I glanced over my shoulder and saw that the way was immediately clear behind me, but I would soon get to a small range of cliffs that I would have to navigate.

I might have been fast, but the lurker was faster. While I was tempted to spread my toes further apart to increase my speed, I decided to make a course correction so that I faced forward. If the lurker caught up to me before I was done, so be it. Roth had said I could fight in hand-to-hand combat with the lurkers, but I did not want to do that if I could avoid it.

I wished that Roth had taught me how to use the propulsion system, instead of just showing me how it worked and saying that it was time to go.

"Suit, what are your commands?"

There was no response.

Of course.

I pushed my toes down and shot up into the sky, not stopping until I gained an altitude of about a thousand feet. I could see what Roth had meant by saying that in the heat of battle, the sharp responsiveness of the suit was desirable. The lurker was far enough back that it looked like an insect, but it had already adjusted its course to intercept me.

"Roth, what is going on? Are you still alive?"

There was still no response.

While I was trying to decide what to do next, I noticed the ship had engaged its evasive maneuvers once again, even though I was no longer inside.

I let out a mirthless chuckle as I studied the lurker. It was no use wishing that Roth had taught me how to use the weapons.

"Suit, activate weapons."

There was no response.

"Activate weapons."

Again nothing.

"Fire a laser at that lurker over there."

Nothing.

I tried the buttons in front of my hands, pushing them at random, but nothing happened.

Figures, they have probably been deactivated.

I had to find Roth, it was the only way.

I turned and sped off in the direction I had last seen Roth going when she had disappeared off the radar.

The lurker was close on my heels.

29

I spread my heels apart as much as I dared, figuring that I had probably reached the suit's top speed. It might have seemed fast in training, but I wished for more speed now that I was sure the lurker was almost to me.

A lot more speed.

The propulsion system would come in real handy right about now.

I tried to turn my head to look behind and found that it automatically adjusted my feet and sent me into a long arc, taking me off the straight course I had planned but also giving me a look behind.

The lurker was several hundred feet back and closing fast, especially now that I had veered off course. I readjusted, opening my heels up as far as I could.

I wasn't going fast enough.

I had only seconds, if that.

I pushed my toes down and shot up in the air. The speed had seemed impossibly fast during my instruction with Roth, but all I could think now was that I was going too slow.

I waited for the count of twenty to give the lurker time to readjust to my move and then spread my feet apart, sinking like a meteor.

I counted to sixty and repeated the process, glad the lurker had not yet caught up to me.

The next time I went up, I spread my toes apart and flew backward, passing the lurker who adroitly flipped in the air to adjust to my maneuver.

It's like death on wings.

Cursing at how skillfully it moved, I pressed my toes down and shot up into the air again, putting my toes together and spreading my heels apart to fly forward.

The maneuver had cost me. The lurker was now that much closer.

I spread my feet apart and sunk down again, expecting that at any moment I was going to feel the lurker reaching out to grab me.

I went so far down that I was mere feet above the ground, zigzagging to the left and then the right to avoid a rock, and then something that looked like a dead tree.

After several moments, I slammed my toes down and fired up.

I continued to do my crazy evasive maneuvers, but the motion was jarring. I could only hope that if the lurker was getting close to me again, I was making it harder for it to catch me.

Unlikely, not for something that's been flying since birth.

"Roth, come in."

There was no response.

I had just come down from a long drop when I saw another lurker on the ground. I assumed at first that this was one she had killed and was just adjusting my course to go around anyway when it jumped into the air and came to meet me. There was a long black mark down its back as if it had been hit by Roth.

I'm getting close.

Where is she?

I turned and went a direction that was perpendicular to the one I had been going before, heading away from where I expected to find Roth but avoiding the creature.

Blasts of light shot past me on either side.

I pushed my toes down and sprung up into the sky in a wide arc, I then spread my feet apart and fell. A moment later, I brought them together and put my toes down and went up like a rocket.

During all the maneuvers, the blue blasts followed me but had gone wildly past. I figured my temporary evasive maneuvers were working, but there was a limit to how long I could go on like this. Roth had said something about the anti-gravs working as long as there was juice in the suit, but I didn't know how much I was using, or how long it would last. I needed a better plan than running.

How long will it be before one hits me with a lucky shot?

I have to fight.

Or wait until one caught me and ripped me to shreds.

I thought again about fighting hand-to-hand in the suit against the lurkers.

Another last resort, one I was loath to try.

I spread my heels apart while swinging one leg out, so I zoomed around in a half-circle like a figure skater on ice until I faced the lurkers. Then, I pushed my toes down and shot up into the air while also spreading my heels, flying upward at a sharp angle.

The lurkers responded just as nimbly as ever. The only advantage was that I appeared to be faster in the moment. I could turn on a dime and propel myself like a rocket, whereas they took a few moments to get back up to speed.

The lurkers were still coming for me when I saw a mountain range in the distance.

I spread my heels and headed towards it.

30

It was only by some miracle that I managed to get to the mountain range without being caught. I continued my evasive maneuvers throughout the trip, expecting that they would either hit me or catch me, forcing a confrontation. I didn't know what would happen when I punched them with my suited hand, but I was prepared to find out when it came to that. I zoomed into the mountains at full speed, trusting that my ability to turn and zip away would be the only thing that would allow me an advantage on the lurkers.

I was not naïve enough to think that I could switch direction at the last moment and send the lurkers careening to their death, but I was going to try. At the very least, I hoped to escape or lose them somehow.

A narrow ravine opened up in front of me just as I came down from a jump of a thousand feet. It felt like the lurkers were breathing on me—I was sure it was just my imagination, but I wasn't going to find out—so I dropped down into it, hoping that it wouldn't get any narrower. It was seven feet wide, if that. My suit was just shy of five with my arms tucked in, so I was taking a risk.

It's this, or have them get me from behind.

The ravine veered to the left. I followed for another hundred feet before it came to a sudden end. That's when I sprung into the air and nearly crashed into a rock ledge I had not seen, only narrowly avoiding it at the last moment by throwing one leg out and shooting off in the other direction. This was something I did on instinct, but I made a mental note as it would be a useful thing to have in my tool chest.

I glanced back, the lurkers had followed without a problem.

They had not fit into the ravine, so they had stayed just above, monitoring what I was doing.

Cursing, I stabilized and veered around a cliff that had come out of nowhere, thinking that my great idea to come here had not been so good after all when I saw them navigate it so easily. It had been one thing to go through the mountains at the speed the transport could move, but it was quite another to do this with only the suit for protection while the lurkers breathed down my neck. Another narrow ravine opened up in the middle of a mountain, so I headed straight for it. This was even smaller than the last, but I hurtled in at full speed, my eyes closing for just a second as I feared I was about to run into a cliff wall. I made it in just fine but kept thinking that my suit was about to clip one side of the wall or the other and send me careening out of control. At the last moment, right before it narrowed to an impossible size, I shot straight up, going headfirst into one of the lurkers. I caught it off guard as much as it surprised me. I was tempted to just push down my toes and get out of there, but I reached out instead and grabbed one of its wings and yanked, trying to tear it off. It felt like it was made from metal.

Still holding onto the wing, I pummeled it with my other hand, but it was like attacking a rock. The suit kept me from feeling any pain, so I kept at it while the lurker tried to bring its small arms around to fire its weapons at me. All the shots went wild.

An idea occurred to me. I acted on it without a second thought. Still keeping hold of the wing, I launched myself up and landed on top of the lurker like I was riding a horse. Then I grabbed the other wing and held on for dear life.

"Turnabout is fair play, you monster," I said, thinking of how one of these lurkers had taken hold of my ship. I just rode for a moment and took advantage of my new position, checking behind on the status of the other lurker. It was about fifty feet back and inching its way closer. The barrage of fire died down, but only for a moment. The lurker resumed shooting at me, heedless of the one underneath. When I faced forward, I tightened my hold as it veered away to avoid running into a cliff, even pushing my foot out to help send us out of its way. As I did, it occurred to me that I could use the anti-gravs to mess up the lurker's flight.

When I spread my feet apart, we lurched downward. The lurker made a sound that I could only describe as a roar in response.

A smile crept across my face.

31

The lurker had not been bothered by me before, but it now tried to buck me off like a high-speed bucking bronco with wings, weapons, and all the terror of a real-life monster. I held on for my life, clinging to the wings and wondering what would happen if I suddenly pushed my toes down and shot upward. Would I pull the lurker with me or rip off its wings?

Time to find out, I thought, slamming my toes down and almost flying off the lurker. My feet went up, but my hands retained their hold on the lurker's wings.

It was gratifying to hear a tearing noise and another roar from the lurker. Using the wings to pull my body down, I repositioned so my legs were once again on either the side of the lurker. Just as I was about to press my toes down again, the lurker dove, flipped to one side and tried to scrape me off with a passing rock.

At the last moment, I brought up a foot and pushed us back just before I would've smacked into the rock.

No more of that, sucker.

I pushed my toes down and lurched upward again. This time I had the satisfying experience of pulling off the wings.

The lurker's scream echoed through the rock canyon. In my exuberance for having accomplished my desire, I ran smack into a cliff and bounced off, spinning away with my feet flying over my head.

I would have expected such a maneuver to send me flying out of control, but it appeared the suit was smart enough to keep that from happening. I was not hurt. A quick glance at my suit told me that it seemed to be okay.

The lurkers had overshot me when I had gone up. The one whose wings I had taken charged with a furious roar, the full effect of which was muted by my suit. I pushed off the cliff and headed straight towards the lurker, wielding its wings like they were oversized spears to agitate the creature. I wished that I could activate my propulsion system. I wanted to see what would happen when I rammed one at full speed. I was confident that my suit would handle the impact without a problem, considering how I had bounced off a cliff and didn't even feel bruised.

Right before we collided, I lurched up a hundred feet, came back down, intending to land on the creature like I had before, but it snaked out of the way at the last moment, turning on me and firing with its blasters. One of the shots went right into my chest but was absorbed, my suit briefly lighting up as it did.

Roth had not explained the suit's defense mechanisms, but she had mentioned it had a shield. It didn't take a genius to figure out that it was a force field that protected me, similar to the transport ship.

By that time, the other lurker was attacking as well. I spread my feet so I fell down into the cliffs, the side of one mere inches from my face. The wounded lurker tried to follow and rammed headfirst into the rock. The other turned away just in time and disappeared behind a rock face.

Smiling, I shot up and landed on the wounded lurker before it knew what I was doing. I grabbed another set of wings and pushed up. I expected that it wasn't going to work yet, so I immediately came back down, pushing up again the second time and tearing off two more wings.

The loss of the first set of wings had not done much to its ability to maneuver, but this time it did. It had one remaining set of wings, and while it could still fly, it lurched in the air as if it had difficulty maintaining its balance.

I lunged onto the top of the creature, landing just behind its head. I brought both my fists into the side of its head, pounding it with all the force I could muster, trusting that the suit would amplify it. It roared but was helpless to do anything about my attack. Its blasters were now firing in all different directions, but nothing came close to hitting me. I bashed it in the head again, jumped off, and landed right behind its other wings. I grabbed hold, but before I could push down with my feet, it twisted and sent me right into the face of the cliff, jarring my head.

I pushed off the cliff with my arm and was surprised at how much strength I had, it sent us twenty feet out. I pushed down with my feet, but the wings did not come. I did it again a second and third time but they still did not go. The lurker writhed and turned every which way, it felt like I was riding a snake. Its maneuvers made it difficult to repeat what I had done before. Finally, I grabbed hold of just one of the wings and pushed down with my toes, sending me up like a speeding bullet with one of its remaining wings. As I went up, the lurker went down in a spiral, bouncing off rock cliffs and outcroppings.

The other lurker had disappeared.

I tossed aside the wing and jumped down after the wounded lurker.

32

It did not occur to me until I was halfway down the cliff, moving to avoid an outcropping, that there was no real need for me to follow the lurker. By the time I had fully processed my action, I had landed right beside it on the ground, crouching to withstand the full force of my landing as I had not made proper use of the anti-gravs to slow down. It roared as it charged.

Roth had been adamant I could fight these things using just my suit so I decided to give it a shot, particularly since I had already damaged this one. It seemed like an excellent learning opportunity to figure out any other weaknesses and vulnerabilities they might have.

I stood my ground—rather than doing the smart thing which would've been to hop into the air and leave—before I ran forward into the enraged lurker, bashing its head with a fist and using my other hand to grab hold of one of its short appendages in front. It twisted its head and tried to bite my arm, but by that time, I was already leaping into the air, easily ripping off the arm I had taken hold of. The jaws of the lurker just missed my feet as I spun away.

I looked down at what I had taken. The appendage had three fingers and held a small weapon that was made so two fingers could hold it while the third fired a trigger that was in the middle.

At least I finally know what its weapon looks like.

It was surprising that this part of the body was so vulnerable when every other bit was well protected, perhaps the creatures figured a good offense was the best defense.

Or maybe they just never had the experience of somebody getting close enough to start ripping things off.

It would have been interesting to take this back, particularly if I connected up with Roth so I could prove to her that I had indeed taken down a lurker, but I had no pockets or another way to store something in my suit, at least not of which I was aware.

I flung the hand in one direction and pointed the blaster at the lurker, but my massive gloved hands were unable to pull the trigger. I crushed it and sent it in the opposite direction of the hand.

While I had hung fifty feet in the air examining the appendage, the lurker had scrambled up a large rock. It was too late by the time I saw what it was doing.

It jumped, crashing into me and pushing me up against the cliff. Cursing, I pushed it away with one hand and shot up into the air. Somehow, it managed to take hold of the rock cliff. It didn't even hesitate before it made another jump at me, but this time I backed out of its way and watched as it landed with a thud on the ground. It was immediately on its feet, roaring and lashing out with its claws. It seemed to be challenging me to a duel, seeming to dare me to meet it on the ground.

When I made no move, it reared back on its hind legs, its remaining hands firing its blasters. The shots were all erratic at first, but they honed in on my position as if the creature was taking control of its fury. Even though I knew the suit's shield could withstand a blast, I did my best to avoid the enemy fire because I didn't want to learn the hard way how resistant the suit was to their weapons. I zipped around, forcing it off its hind legs so that it could follow me before it bounced back up on them and started firing again. Strangely, the first several shots were once again erratic before it could aim at me. I removed its remaining wing while we continued the dance. If it was furious before, it was worse now.

I repeated the maneuver several more times, slowly lowering until I was close enough that it could jump up and get me. Each time it bounced back up on its legs, it was difficult for it to reacquire me as a target. I counted the last time, it took three seconds to hone in on me.

I might have said something taunting to the creature, but Roth had not taught me how to speak other than on the radio.

"Roth, Roth, are you there?"

There was no answer.

I studied the creature, skating out of the way whenever it tried to fire at me, hoping to think of a way to dispatch it. I looked around for a boulder or something that I might push on top of it, but there was nothing nearby. Whenever I got close enough to punch its head, the move had bothered the creature, but it only seemed to infuriate it and had not done any harm.

It lunged for me, and I casually pushed down my toes, launching fifty feet up into the air, spinning as I did. As the suit gave me additional strength, I wondered just how big of a rock I could pick up. I saw a likely candidate in the next canyon over and went down. When I tried to pick it up, I discovered it was heavier than I had judged. I could barely get my arms around it. Regardless, I tried one side and found that I could tip it over without much effort.

I couldn't find a way to lift it.

Unfortunately, it was the only nearby rock that had a chance of damaging the lurker. All the rest were too large or just small enough to irritate it.

How fast can I throw them?

I picked up several of the smaller rocks and flew back over to the other side, where I found that the lurker had been climbing again. I skated backward while I wound up my arm and flung a rock. It would've killed a person, but I might as well have just thrown a pebble because it bounced harmlessly off.

The creature kept climbing, stopping only to roar at me.

I hesitated but only for a moment and spread my feet and heels at the same time, dropping while flying forward. I grabbed one of its hindlegs, thinking that maybe I could rip it off like I had the wing, and shot up into the air. When the lurker realized what I had done, it turned and snatched at me, trying to bite my arms and losing its hold on the rock at the same time.

I came to a halt, holding the creature by one leg. I then pushed my toes down, and surprisingly, the whole creature came with me. I did not move as fast, but it was quick enough that we were soon several hundred feet in the air.

I kept going up while the creature tried to get me.

Higher and higher we went. The lurker became increasingly agitated the further we got from the ground.

There had to be a point where the lurker would die when I dropped it.

We were soon at a thousand feet, and then we passed two thousand, but I still did not stop. I lost track of time as I slowly spun in the air, looking for signs of the other lurker, wondering if it would come to the aid of its companion, but other then some clouds, the sky was clear. The transport was also long gone.

The lurker stopped squirming. I glanced down. Had it lost consciousness?

It had curled into a ball so that its jaws were now mere feet from my legs. It was trying to stretch further but appeared to be at the limit of what it could do.

How high am I? Fifteen thousand feet? Twenty?

I was tempted to let go but still continued to rise. I doubted it had the leverage necessary to come around and clamp onto me. I wanted to make sure that when I let go, it had no chance of surviving.

Just when I was thinking of releasing it, I heard a noise behind me and turned to see that the other lurker had been hiding in a cloud.

Without realizing what I was doing, I let go of the lurker's leg and did not even watch as it plummeted toward the ground.

33

The falling lurker screamed, but the sound disappeared from my consciousness as I focused on the oncoming monster that roared, approaching like a speeding train.

Blasts of light from its weapons went by on either side while I thought about my next best course of action.

Now is the real test. I've shown that I can kill a lurker that's been wounded, assuming it dies when it hits the ground. How do I take one on in full health?

It occurred to me that the lurker's aim was not very good. While I had considered my options, none of the blasts had come anywhere close to me, probably because I was still moving upward after letting go of the lurker. I was going fast, but the lurker was still a good distance out, so my movement should not have made a big difference in its aim.

I am a sitting duck.

The lurkers had been deadly with their blasters back at camp. Why couldn't this lurker hit me?

Had it been wounded by Roth?

It should have hit me at least a couple times, but none of the blasts had even come close, it was as if the purpose of its blasts were just to distract me. I had not felt any danger and had taken no evasive maneuvers to get out of its line of fire.

Is it just hoping to keep me pinned down?

Just as the lurker was about to reach me, it suddenly wrapped its wings behind its back and dove. On instinct, I spread my toes, sliding back before I realized that the lurker was not coming for me.

It was going after the lurker I had just dropped.

I was surprised at the lurker's desire to save his comrade, particularly since it had fired at me while I'd been riding the other like a space cowboy. I spread my feet apart, plummeting after it. I was curious about what it was doing.

A lurker focused on rescuing another is just as distracted as one without wings. It was another opportunity to use the suit in direct combat that I could not pass up.

It was strange to fall like that without any type of parachute. The suit's amazing technology that made me feel like I was in my body while wearing a suit gave me the strangest sensation of falling. I experienced a brief wave of fear as I started to wonder if maybe I had imagined it all and would also hit the ground with the lurkers.

Regardless, I continued to fall, not moving my feet a millimeter.

I wanted to see what the lurker would do. I wanted to learn how it would save its companion. As it looked like I was about to be alone amongst all these lurkers, it seemed prudent to learn anything about their psychology that I could.

The lurker's wings moved in full force, forcing it towards its falling comrade. The wounded lurker had its legs spread wide to increase its drag.

Was I witnessing something they practiced in training?

I shook my head as I got closer. I had not expected these creatures to have a sense of loyalty towards each other.

It almost made them seem human.

Another thought occurred to me and I was surprised that it was only now that I made this observation.

I was falling faster than I should have.

I spread my legs even farther, increasing my speed.

I had disrupted the lurker while riding it and doing the same thing.

How had I missed that?

It was not exactly the propulsion system I had seen Roth use, but it was something more than just mere gravity that propelled me downward because I soon caught up to the lurker that was trying to rescue its comrade.

It did not see me coming.

As much as I wanted to see how this played out, I could not pass up an opportunity to attack while it was focused elsewhere.

I maneuvered until I was right beside it. I glanced down, it was still not aware of my presence. I grabbed a wing that moved so fast it looked like it was barely there, clasping it between two hands with a snapping motion and then bracing myself against its body, trying to rip it off.

I would use the antigravity feature as a last resort to shoot up in the air, but I wanted to stay close to the lurker to maximize my ability to damage it before it turned on me.

The lurker went into a spin. I tried to maintain a hold but was sent flying off with its wing. As soon as I was off the spinning creature, I righted myself, thanks to the aid of the suit's anti-gravs, leaving me holding the wing that I had torn off.

The creature screamed but made no move toward me, it had still not caught up to the falling lurker and was slower now that it had one less wing.

It's anybody's guess if it will catch the other before it hits the ground.

The margin of error was not significant, if he was to save his companion, he could not even spend one moment dealing with me. I repositioned, grabbed another wing, and waited until the lurker started twisting again before I flew off with the wing in hand.

By the time I was back at the lurker, it had spun around so that its feet faced towards me. As I maneuvered to try to go around, it followed, keeping me from getting to its wings.

Now would be a really good time to know how to use the weapons.

"Activate weapons."

Nothing.

"Roth, are you there?"

Nothing.

With every passing attempt to reach out to her, I knew the chances of us reconnecting were slim. I had a hard time believing these creatures had managed to kill her, particularly when the suit was so adept at fighting them, but I was starting to think that I needed to accept she might be gone.

When I thought of the tough woman who I could only describe as half crazy, I felt remorse at the thought she might be dead.

While I didn't trust her and probably never would, I did like her.

I pretended to go left, but then went right, and soon found myself taking hold of another of the lurker's wings while stabilizing my feet on its back. Instead of spinning around like it had before, it remained still, clearly having figured out that its actions had done more damage to it than I had.

When I tried to rip it off, two other wings were suddenly in front of me, buzzing right in my face. This did not have any effect on me, other than to disorient me just a little, but I grabbed hold of another wing and pulled on two at once. Unfortunately, this made me lose my stance on the back of the creature, and I was soon dangling off, holding only the wings.

It seemed like I was holding on to save my life, but after a moment of reflection I realized I could just let go. It was difficult to do but was not really any different than getting tossed by the creature. As soon as I did I immediately righted myself.

Whoever designed this suit had aerial maneuvers in mind.

I spread my feet and caught up to the lurker.

It rotated so its feet faced towards me once again. A hand with a blaster pointed at me and I moved to the left. It did not follow me.

Was it just my imagination or had the wings increased in speed?

The lurker pulled ahead in its descent toward the ground and I spread my feet to keep up.

The ground was coming quick, I didn't know how long we had before I needed to pull up, but it was seconds away.

The lurker pulled forward even further, it wings going so fast I had a hard time imagining how it was even possible.

I hesitated but only for a second before I spread my feet.

The wounded lurker cried out like it was pleading for help. I felt bad for the creature's plight, but I pushed the thought away because I could not afford to think like that. These things would kill me the moment they had an opportunity.

It was them or me.

I choose me.

The lurker put on a sudden burst of speed, closing a distance of about fifty feet until it was just a few feet away from the wounded lurker.

I hung back, not wanting to get caught in something if these two wound up in a tangle and went down.

The wounded lurker turned so that it's back was to the ground and its legs were up. The other lurker repositioned so its legs faced those of the wounded lurker. They wrapped their legs around each other and then the lurker started pumping its wings, trying to pull out of their death spiral.

I landed on top of the lurker and grabbed a wing in each hand, causing the lurker to roar. I was perfectly positioned for the maneuver I had done before so without a moment of hesitation, I launched into the air.

Just like before, they didn't come off easily, but after a couple tries, there was a tearing sound and I managed to altogether remove them from the lurker.

The creature cried out and the remaining wings suddenly increased in speed again. The lurker fought a losing battle now it only had two wings left.

I looked down at the ground and at the lurkers, wondering if I dared go in for yet another move. They were both likely to die at this rate, but I wanted to make sure they did not survive.

The lurker twisted, its eyes focusing on me as I came down and landed on top of him. It tried to hit me with its blasters, but every shot missed. I grabbed one of the remaining good wings and launched myself upward, the wing coming off far easier than I had expected. My guess was the tension of carrying the extra weight of the other lurker, plus the fatigue from moving far faster than normal, had made them more pliable.

It was difficult to describe my feelings.

Elation.

Regret.

I was overwhelmed that I'd managed to do all the things I had done. I hated what I had done, but did not see another way out. I'd had an opportunity to kill these lurkers and I had taken it.

The lurker on the bottom pushed away from the lurker on top, spun, and went into a dive, clearly making sure that the remaining lurker did not try again to save it.

That final wing beat hard, slowing the lurker more than I would've expected possible.

The screams of the lurker below stopped when it hit the ground head first, it would not get up again.

Relief flooded through me. The horror was gone. Now that the monster was dead, I did not regret it.

The remaining lurker, for a brief moment, looked like it was about to fly, but then it managed to land in a tumble of claws that ended in a roll.

I came down beside it, landing softer than I had ever done in any of my previous attempts with the anti-grav boots or the suit.

The lurker charged.

I stood my ground, even though we were on an open desert plain with nothing around for me to use as a defense.

I got this.

<h1 style="text-align:center">34</h1>

A blast of light came out of nowhere and tore the lurker in two pieces, sending the parts skidding to a halt fifty feet in front of me. It took me a moment to realize what had happened before a sense of unfulfilled expectations flowed through me, which was surprising because the problem had been so easily resolved. I had been confident I could handle this lurker as well, considering how I had taken care of the last one.

It felt like the opportunity to prove myself had been taken away, but I shook it off.

I fought two lurkers and survived, using only my suit and wits, even killing one without the suit's weapons. That's not nothing.

"When I said you could fight hand-to-hand with the lurkers, I meant that more figuratively, not literally."

Relief flowed through me to hear Roth's voice.

"I really said it to keep you from demanding that I teach you how to use the weapons. They can be tricky, and it's easy to do the wrong thing." She chuckled. "I should've known you'd take me at my word."

Irritation flowed through me, but I swept it away. It helped that I had been successful at something she had said just to satiate me.

"Where have you been? I've been trying to reach you."

"How did you take down these two lurkers by yourself?"

Roth now hovered above me in the air.

"One. You got the second. How long have you been watching?"

"I just barely got here. I saw that guy over there take a nosedive into the ground and the other guy that came down with only one wing..." She trailed off. "Did you remove their wings? That is impressive. How high up did you go?"

"I have no idea. We fell for quite some time, so probably higher than I thought. I ripped off the wings because I figured that was the only way I could fight them."

"I don't know that anybody's ever tried that."

"Really?"

"No, but I guess everybody usually has weapon's training, so there isn't a need." Roth shook her head. "The suits are only rated for ten thousand feet, we teach soldiers to not go above five. Did you see a flashing light out the corner of your eye?"

I thought back and shook my head. "Not that I can recall. I was pretty focused at the time."

"You are one merciless man."

"It was them or me."

"Don't mistake me, you did the right thing. It's just…" She trailed off again but did not finish her thought. "How did you get into the suit? Didn't I deactivate it before I left?"

I shrugged, but I doubted that it came through while in the suit. "I activated it."

Roth shook her head. "Just when I think you're too big of a screwup, you do something like this that makes me want to keep you around."

"Terrible shame, that. What comes next?"

"What happened to the ship?" Roth asked as she landed.

"I dunno." I pointed in the direction it had gone. "Last I saw it was still going that way. Unless it ran into more lurkers, it's probably still going that same direction. Do you think we can catch it?"

"Not without me teaching you to use the full propulsion system, and I'm not gonna do that. We don't have enough time."

"You'll have to teach me sometime."

"Yes, it's far trickier than your suit's antigravity. It seems like you have managed that well enough, so it bodes well when I do have an opportunity to teach you. We're talking about hours, not minutes."

"You saw what I could do with the bare knowledge you imparted. Do you want real help when we go into Camp Myers?"

"Yes, but we don't have the time it'll take for me to bring you up to speed. That was gutsy of you to jump out of a moving ship. Did you have any problems?"

I thought back to how difficult it had been to activate the suit and was tempted to make a snarky remark but resisted the desire.

"It was okay once I got into the suit. I didn't really have much choice. I had to bail out. One of the lurkers had fastened on top of the ship, and it kept the ship from making evasive maneuvers. I tried to access the ship's controls, but it looked like you locked them out." She nodded to indicate my assessment was correct. Her suit head didn't move, it was the projection on her helmet. "It was cutting in with a saw."

"That happens from time to time."

"You still haven't told me where you've been."

"The last one I fought was a tough sucker, I'm not quite sure I killed it, but at least it's temporarily down." She jerked a hand back toward the mountains where I had been frolicking with the lurkers. "I was back there. The thing was talented, I'll say that much. Okay, are you ready?"

"No." I shook my head emphatically. "Teach me how to use the weapons." Roth hesitated like she was gonna say no. I stepped towards her. "Doesn't it count for something that I managed to take two down with my bare hands."

"One, I got the other."

"I was about to finish it off, you know it. I think you can trust me with a weapon. It doesn't have to be all of them, just teach me one simple weapon. I need the ability to point and bring them down. Wouldn't you rather I can point and kill instead of having to jump on their back to pop off wings. That's gonna be a far worse distraction and maybe even cost us more time in the long run."

"I suppose I owe you that much." She brought up her right hand. "I told you not to touch any of the buttons that were in front of your hand. Did you try any of them?"

"Maybe once or twice."

A sly smile crossed her face. "I never activated them, so even if you pressed them, nothing happened."

I just nodded without saying anything, remembering the frustration and anger I felt at having to fight the lurkers without anything I could use to destroy them.

"I will activate one of the weapons. There is a trigger in front of the index finger on your right hand. Point it at one of the dead lurkers and pull it."

"You mean just aim my hand?"

"Yes."

I brought it up and held it in the direction of the severed body of a lurker, the legs of which still moved, and then pulled the trigger.

Nothing happened.

"Are you sure you activated it?"

"Yes. You have to hold it down for five seconds."

I thought you were in a hurry, why didn't you mention that before?

I depressed the trigger again and held it down, there was no visible indication that I was doing anything. I had expected a beam of light, similar to what she had used to tear the nearly wingless lurker in half, but nothing came.

A moment later a high-pitched screeching came from the lurker's body. The hardened shell I was pointing at began to smoke before it burst into flame, an explosion coming right afterward.

"Can I kill them on first contact without having to wait five seconds?"

"No, but if you aim for the head it will mess with their mind until their skull explodes. They probably will not hold still long enough for that. You still might have to jump on their back and rip off wings." Roth leaped into the air. "We have wasted too much time, let's go."

I gritted my teeth as I jumped and followed her.

35

The forward movement of the anti-gravs seemed to increase our speed the longer we used them. We were only several hundred feet in the air, so the ground speeding beneath our feet seemed to pass far faster than it had in the transport. Before too long, we were over the spot where I had abandoned the ship. It came and went in a blur.

If I'd have known that the longer I held this position, the faster I would go, I might've just tried to outrun them. Perhaps in this instance, ignorance had been to my benefit.

It would've been a mistake to run, so I was glad I had not tried. The experience I had just come through was valuable, and I had survived without a scratch. Not only was it a confidence builder, but there was nothing like first-hand experience to truly learn something.

Roth maintained radio silence for most of our journey, I didn't know if this was for a strategic purpose or just because she was focused on getting to Camp Myers.

Even though we had moved faster on the ship, I preferred how we currently traveled. For one, I felt far more secure because I was not putting my life solely into Roth's hands. For another, it was far more engaging, so I was fully alert. If we encountered more lurkers, I was in a better position to deal with them in every way possible.

Another mountain range slowly grew up ahead until it took up most of the horizon. Roth headed straight for it.

"We must keep a low profile from here on out. While I am tempted to just hop over the mountains, I think we should go through while staying as low as we can go to avoid detection. Camp Myers is just on the other side. Stay close."

We hurtled into the mountain range at full speed. I had no idea how fast we were going, but it felt unsafe. I had never been much of a speed demon back on earth, but my experiences here had started to bring on an adrenaline rush. The full protection of the suit helped me enjoy the experience. This was far better than when we had relied on the transport to take us through the mountains.

Roth turned a corner around a cliff and leaped up in the air. I followed on instinct before I saw that a hill was coming our way. It seemed like the bottoms of my feet were going to scrape, but I cleared just fine.

I gawked at what I saw on the other side.

For the first time since coming here, I actually saw a stream of running water at the bottom of a canyon. It was small and no more than several feet wide. Judging by the surrounding area and vegetation, it did not look like it had ever been any bigger. Green grass and small plants grew beside the stream. I even saw a creature that looked like a deer, but it came and went so fast I did not have time to fully appreciate it.

It was difficult to not stare at the running water, but I kept my eyes forward, continuing to glance down every now and again to be sure that it was still there. It was strange how such a little thing could have an effect on me.

A few minutes later, after we'd zipped around several other cliffs and hopped over some low hanging peaks, a vast, impossibly tall cliff emerged ahead of us at the end of the ravine we currently traveled through. The cliff ran in either direction with a rock wall on the opposite sides, forming steep canyons to our right and left. At first, I wondered if this was a man-made wall, but then as I looked closer, I saw the distinct breaks and crags in the rockface. Based on what Roth had said earlier about keeping a low profile, I expected that she would turn, but she went straight forward toward the cliff.

"We have to go up," she said a moment later, "despite the fact the cliff is tall. Once we get near the top we are going to slow down. We can't afford to be seen now so follow my lead."

We stopped twenty feet back from the cliff and began to climb. Rather than shoot up like Roth had before, she took this at a steady speed.

As we moved, I began to grow uncomfortable, though I could not explain why. It felt like somebody was watching us. I kept my eyes peeled, scanning the area around us as best I could, but saw nothing to indicate there was anything to my fears.

When I saw movement to the left, I turned, afraid that a lurker was about to attack, but instead, I saw the tip of a grenling's head peeking out from the mouth of a cave deep in the cliff. Then I saw another, peeking around from a rock outcropping a hundred feet away from where we were. This one looked small, like it was a child.

"We're not alone up here."

"No."

Her tone told me she already knew this and that there was more than she had said, but she did not want to get into it. I turned at a movement on our right, but it was gone before I could make it out. I did not need a good look to know it was another grenling.

"This is a grenling colony," Roth said as she turned and flew to the right. "We will be past it momentarily. No need to panic." After going several hundred feet over, she started to climb again.

She had known about this beforehand? Why hadn't she told me? I ground my teeth at the withheld knowledge but kept my mouth shut. *Hadn't I already proven myself?*

She could trust me with necessary information.

There was scraping on the rocks down below, and Roth pushed faster. I was happy to follow her lead.

We were only halfway up the cliff when a grenling came out above us, peeking its head over the top of a protruding ledge, it's helmet glinting in the light of day.

"How hard is it to kill a grenling compared to a lurker?"

"A little bit easier. They are not nearly as menacing, nowhere near as smart, and the weapons, as you've seen, are primitive. But that isn't the problem. If we fight them, it will give away our presence. Camp Myers is just on the other side of this mountain. This might not be an issue if the battle is still underway, but it might be that everybody's either dead or evacuated, and that will immediately draw the lurker's wrath." She glanced over, the image looking weird as it was projected against the side of her helmet. "That's why we didn't go around even though this place is infested with grenlings, our best shot is up and over. Camp Myers keeps a watch around the clock to make sure grenlings don't invade the camp, but something tells me they're out of commission today." She shook her head. "All the activity must've woken the grenlings, they tend to be nocturnal." She went to the left a hundred feet, I followed after.

I looked up at the towering cliff and saw nothing. The grenlings were there, they were all just hiding. I looked down and saw a dozen climbing up towards us. When I looked up again, there were five heading down.

Others came from all directions.

36

Jeffords had mentioned that grenlings were terrific climbers. I saw now that this was the case as I spread my toes and pushed back from the cliff on instinct, while Roth did the same. Unfortunately, we couldn't go much further back than fifty feet because of the other rock wall right behind us that ran parallel up to almost the full height of the cliff we were climbing.

Roth and I continued up along the wall as the grenlings closed in. The ones from above were the closest and within seconds were parallel with us. These creatures were astonishing, hopping around on the rocks like they were mountain goats with hands and opposable thumbs.

They moved with us. This still wasn't much of a problem because we were out of distance of their clubs. Unless they started throwing them like missiles, we'd be okay. And even if they did, it shouldn't be too hard to dodge them. They did not have a good position on the rockface to throw the clubs like they had back in camp.

"How worried should I be?" I asked.

Roth didn't answer, but her lips had formed a thin concentrated line.

I had thought that the club strapped to their backs were their only weapons, but I now saw slings as well. One of the nearby grenlings stopped moving and held on with a clawed hand while using the other to spin a sling with a rock the size of a boulder. That grenling was soon joined by five more.

Roth increased her speed but only by a small margin. I wanted to just shoot up to the top of the cliff, but maintained my course, trusting that she knew what she was doing and that my desire to just haul up to the top was dangerous.

A hail of rocks came our way.

Roth didn't budge, so I maintained my position as well, bringing up my hands and batting away the first couple boulders until there were too many to protect against all of them. Most bounced harmlessly off my suit, but one large one knocked me back, almost sending me careening into the rock wall behind us. I managed to shake it off, just like when I had run into the cliff wall in my fight with the lurker. The damage was slight and I was soon back on course beside Roth.

The grenlings called out, saying something that I could not understand. To my ears, it sounded like a bunch of growls and groans, but to somebody trained in such things, they might have appeared to be communicating in a language of some sort.

During our battle with the grenlings at camp, I hadn't heard them do anything other than roar. Even though I could not make out individual words, I figured that what we heard was the precursor of a developing language for these people.

"Are you sure we shouldn't just speed up?" I asked.

"We'll be fine. Sticks and stones we can deal with. If we show up and the lurkers are waiting for us, things will be much worse."

I shook my head and muttered something inaudible.

"What was that?" Roth asked sharply.

"Nothing."

Another barrage of boulders came our way, I kept a vigilant watch this time, using my feet to skate out of the way while knocking as many away with my hands as I could, but just like before, I was unable to keep them all from hitting me. Several hit my head, and while it did not hurt, the effect was jarring.

"Stop fighting them so much," Roth said as an unusually large boulder bounced off her head. She appeared to be just fine. "The suit protects us. The bigger concern we have right now is what we do when we get to the top. We need a way to keep them from following us."

A large stone hit me in the chest and sent me back into the cliff wall behind me, but I soon regained my balance and maintained my course with Roth. She had been dealing with the boulders too, but I received the brunt of it.

She probably feels the same way.

I shook my head and blinked my eyes to clear them as a new attack began. The grenlings were now gathered and calling at us in frustration, a sort of chant forming that I was sure could be heard from Camp Myers. Their calls grew louder, and I feared the lurkers might come to investigate.

"If they would just leave us alone, I wouldn't hurt them," Roth said, more to herself than to me. "They are going to make us fight them."

"Are these suits equipped for us to fight them in hand-to-hand combat?" I asked, unable to keep the sarcasm from showing.

She just grunted in response, apparently not appreciating my attempt at levity.

"I did not expect so many," she said at length. "I think we approached this wrong. We should have just shot up the cliff and hoped to be well past it before the grenlings came up."

"It's not too late—"

Apparently, Roth was thinking the same thing, because she pushed her toes down and shot up fifty feet before readjusting. I did the same. We managed to get ahead of the grenlings, but only for a few moments. I was surprised she'd only gone so far, instead of the whole way, but before I had a chance to ask her about it, Roth repeated the maneuver, leaving me to catch up. This gave us a little bit of lead on them, one which they quickly closed.

We were fifty feet down from the top of the cliff when Roth came to a halt and turned to me. "We have a dilemma. I can burn enough of these suckers away in a couple minutes to send them all running, but we have a policy to not bother them unless they engage with us. Technically speaking, yes, they are following us, but we stirred them up."

"You want to avoid killing them?" I was surprised at her discretion as she nodded.

"Yes, but I don't see another way around it. If we cross the top of the cliff and they follow, that will only draw the lurker's attention."

"We could outrun them before we go over," I said, pointing to our right. The canyon opened up in that direction, if we went over that way and then shot up, we might get ahead of the grenlings.

"Nice thinking, newbie. It's worth a try." Roth flew to the right as a chorus came up from the grenlings. I followed right after her.

37

Roth increased her speed, going as fast as she had before we reached the mountain range. I was just about ten feet behind her, keeping pace while feeling like we were in a race through a canyon with wild animals chasing us. We left the grenlings behind when we went around a turn. Our plan was working.

"Are we ready to go over?" I asked, looking at the wall to our left and thinking that now was the best time to do it.

"It was a nice thought, but we are going to have to fight our way through."

It took me a moment to realize what she meant. Hundreds of grenlings were in the canyon ahead of us, those on ledges wielded their clubs or readied their slings.

"How can there be so many in such a small space? What do they even eat?" I shook my head. "Should we keep on going and hope we can outrun them?"

"Unfortunately, that's not gonna work. The canyon ends just up there, you can't see it yet, but I've flown over here before, we have maybe another half mile. One way or another we're going up, I will give it a little bit longer to see if we can outrun these guys, but I think we're just gonna have to fight them until they back off."

"A flick of our feet and we'll be higher than they could ever go."

"Negative. We are not going to risk that. As much as I don't want to send a bunch of these guys to their deaths, that's exactly what we have to do."

I let out a sigh, surprised at how adamant I felt about protecting the grenlings despite the way that they had ransacked our camp the day before. "Okay, let's give it a little longer."

Thirty seconds passed and even though we were moving along at quite the speed, it was clear that there were just too many grenlings about. Maybe we had stumbled upon a yearly gathering.

"Are you ready to fight?" Roth asked me.

I didn't relish the idea of more hand-to-hand combat, even with the incredible suit. I imagined them all piling on top of me and taking me captive.

"Any chance you can give me something to actually kill these creatures that doesn't take five seconds?"

Roth just grunted. "On the count of three, we stop and engage."

"One."

We zoomed through the canyon as the number of grenlings seemed to grow, the chant had been taken up by all. I could not tell if the ones that had chased us had caught up, because they would have been lost in a sea of their people.

"Two."

I shook my head, wondering exactly how Roth was going to fight these creatures, but she never got to three. From the cliff on our right, no fewer than a dozen leaped from up above us, several throwing their clubs, making both of us take evasive action so we did not get hit.

One club came within two inches of my face while I had been moving to escape another. It had been going fast enough that I was glad I had not found out if the suit would turn it away.

On instinct, I spread my feet and went down, increasing in speed just like I had with the lurkers before, only this time I did not have as far to fall, I would have to pull up soon. I outpaced the grenlings that aimed for me.

As I came out of my fall and skated forward, I noticed that the closest to me had wings like that of a gliding squirrel and had turned to chase after me.

Are the wings a feature of their suited armor?

I studied one that glided by that was unable to get to me. I decided my assumption was correct. Just like they were covered in armor, some had suits that were made to fly. When I caught a glance of another flying grenling, I realized the armor they wore appeared to be something other than metal.

Leather?

I couldn't tell.

I just could not believe they had not considered them sentient creatures.

Cursing, I changed my direction and shot back towards the grenling, hoping that I could overshoot it before it got to me. It did a somersault in midair and then impossibly reversed course, though not with as much skill as a lurker.

I could take out a lurker, they were far more advanced.

How much harder can a grenling be?

I gritted my teeth.

It's just difficult because they were impossible to fight yesterday. My paradigm had not shifted as easily as I had put on the suit.

I can do this.

Five seconds later, I changed course again and ran into a grenling. It lashed out, its claws wrapping around me as if I were a child, but doing no harm because of the suit. This was once again a weird phenomenon because it felt like I was in my own body, not the suit. There was pressure on my skin where the grenling's claws touched me, but it seemed to just be an indicator that something was touching the suit.

The grenling was more than double my height and broader as well, though not by much. It was lithe while my suit was thick and sturdy, I did not have a clear view of its clawed hands, but it did not look like they wrapped all the way around me. On instinct, I reached up and pushed its head with one of my hands because it was about to take a bite of me, even though I knew there was a helmet between me and the grenling. I brought up my other hand, punching the creature's side and then pulling the trigger.

If the grenling had known what I was up to, it would have pushed me away; instead, it maintained its hold with one claw while trying to get at me with the other.

It was a strange mid-air battle as the anti-gravs kept me in the air and upright, but the forward motion of the grenling sent us backward. If it had not been for my weapon, I would have been using the anti-gravs to escape. Instead, I wanted to be as close to this creature as I could to maintain the requisite hold for five seconds.

When I hit the count of five, the effect was instantaneous. Its fur caught fire, the insides of the grenling gurgled and then blew out the other side opposite of my hand, splattering me with blood while killing the creature. The grenling released its hold and fell to the canyon floor.

I can't believe this suit was underneath our camp the entire time we fought the grenlings and that nobody bothered to bring it out. I expected the reason was that they didn't want to expose us to the suits yet or because they wanted to give us a real-life battle situation as practice.

Regardless, it was reckless they had not handled that situation better.

A large rock bounced off my suit, and I turned to see that the source was a grenling who had flown by and flung it with a sling. Like before, I could feel the pressure on my skin where the rock had hit. I recognized it as a response from the suit to indicate what had happened, not something that was specifically caused by the actual rock.

More rocks were thrown my way, but I ignored all of them unless they got too big. The suit was made to withstand them, and I took full advantage of that protection.

I pushed down with my toes and shot up. When I saw another grenling, I aimed my weapon but was unable to get a fix on it for as long as required.

Not knowing what else to do, and not seeing Roth because of the other flying grenlings that swarmed around us, I charged the closest grenling, latched on, and repeated what I had just done, sending it down to its death. More rocks came my way, and even a club or two, but that was not as common. While I watched, a grenling leaped onto a ledge, scooped up a large rock that it put into a sling, and then jumped off again, heading towards me.

Rather than skate out of the way, I pointed my weapon directly at it and slowed to maintain my aim. Five seconds later, it rippled, and a blast came out of its back. It flew forward but not for long, soon losing control and toppling down into the ravine.

That one had looked younger than the others. I felt a flash of remorse for what I had done, but another grenling came whizzing by, keeping me from focusing on it.

It was an interesting experience to fly with the grenlings because they were not nearly as skilled as the lurkers.

The lurkers had been flying since the day they were born, whereas the grenlings had learned to use their flight suits in the same way I had learned to use mine.

And their technology is not nearly as advanced.

Two down, dozens more to go, I thought as another dozen flying grenlings jumped from the canyon walls on either side of me. It appeared that their strategy was to attack with brute force, kind of like how they had attacked the camp.

"Roth, where are you?"

There was no immediate answer, and for a moment, I wondered if maybe something had happened to her.

"The question is, where did you go?" Roth asked me a moment later.

"I'm deep in the canyon, with these flying grenlings circling overhead. Why didn't anybody tell me they had suits that help them fly?"

"I guess it never came up, did it?"

"And nobody thought to consider them sentient beings?"

"We sent somebody to meet with them early on, but it didn't go well. If they are self-aware beings, and I admit there is evidence that points to that possibility, they certainly don't do themselves any favors. They're probably one of the lowest we've ever encountered."

"What other alien races are there?" I asked.

"Now is not the time to get into that."

There never is a good time to get into anything. I shook my head as I scanned the sky to find Roth. *But she has a point.*

I soon spotted her. She had not lost a foot in altitude and was up there fighting the grenlings. Every now and again I saw a blast of light come from her suit, tearing a grenling in half and sending it to the ground.

"Don't you wish you would've taught me to do that?" I asked as she ripped apart another.

"Where are you?"

"Down about two hundred feet."

"Come back up. Now."

I pushed my toes down, but just as I did, a flying grenling slammed into me, pinning me against the wall.

Then we both fell.

38

To: Brigadier General Katrina Roth
From: Lieutenant General Regina Adams
Log date: 00429.211-14:44:53

Re: The asset

General Roth,

I just received word of the invasion. This should go without saying, but the asset is your highest priority. Please make sure he is protected at all times and evacuated as soon as possible.

I don't want to start over again, we've already lost too much time as it is.

Lieutenant General Regina Adams

39

I tried to right myself by moving my feet, but the anti-gravs were not responding. Why weren't they working? Every time I had been knocked around, the suit had righted itself. Was it because the grenling had a tight hold on me?

Or were the anti-gravs deactivated when I was crushed against the cliff?

Hoping that the suit had not been damaged, I pressed the buttons on my arm and felt them kick in, but we still continued to fall, probably because my feet were in the air and the suit was confused by my present orientation. I tried everything I could to fix that, but nothing seemed to work as the grenling clutched me tight, keeping me from maneuvering.

The grenling shifted. I was now right side up.

I could not see the ground and could only see the grenling, which clawed at me with its other hand as if trying to figure out how to get me out of the suit. It dawned on me that my feet were spread and the velocity of our fall was now increasing. If I didn't do something soon, we would hit the ground at an incredible speed. I couldn't close my feet because the grenling's knee was in the way.

I jammed my hand into the grenling's side, pulled the trigger, and waited. Each second seemed to take forever as I feared we were about to slam into the unforgiving ground. When the weapon finally went off, the stupid grenling did not let go of me even though blood gushed out of its side like a broken dam. Twisting so I had a better view of its arm, I jammed my hand into its arm, pulled the trigger and waited for another eternal five seconds before a gaping hole appeared there. Finally, he released me. The grenling hit the ground with enough force that it seemed to break every bone in the creature's body, regardless of the fact it wore armor.

I came inches from colliding with the bottom of the ravine as I pushed my toes down and shot up into the air.

"Where did you go?" Roth demanded a moment later.

"A grenling jumped on me," I said between gasps for breath, "nearly went down. Coming now." I moved so fast that if I hit another grenling, I was liable to take it down with the force of my upward movement alone.

In moments, I was back in the thick of things. A grenling came right at me, and rather than engaging, I shot forward, looking for Roth.

She was two hundred feet ahead and a hundred feet above me. I closed the distance in time to see her dispatch two grenlings with the laser beam. I gritted my teeth and forced back my anger. I *would* get access to that weapon. The weapon she had given me was nice, but it didn't work nearly as well as the laser. I needed something that was far more responsive if I was gonna help her out.

If she had taught me to use that one, I could've quickly dispatched these creatures instead of resorting to hand-to-hand combat.

"It took you long enough," Roth said, turning so she could see me as I approached. "Are you ready?"

"Sure."

"We never should have come here, it would have been easier to deal with dozens instead of hundreds." There was an accusatory tone to her words that I didn't like.

"You were the one who didn't want to kill them. I just suggested a way to try to avoid that."

"Let's go," Roth said as if she had not heard me.

She darted forward, and I followed after, veering out of the way of a grenling by hopping over without even thinking about the controls.

At least all this activity has given me an instinctual ability to use the suit.

As I passed by above, I brought my hand down and pressed the trigger, but I did not have the time necessary to activate the weapon before my suited arm would no longer follow it. A more skilled soldier could probably have turned and maintained their aim on the creature.

I snorted. *But that soldier would also know how to use the laser.*

The hesitation I'd been feeling about harming these creatures was gone. I was going to kill anything that got in my way.

Roth waited for me beside the cliff, turning every which way to fire that laser beam of hers to keep the grenlings at bay. As I watched, three severed grenlings toppled from the cliff towards the ground like a jumble of broken toys. Strangely, it did not appear the face of the cliff had been harmed by the weapon, even though I was sure it should have cut a broad swath into it.

"Why didn't that thing damage the rock?" I asked.

"We're gonna go up nice and slow," Roth said. "If anything gets too close, you kill it. Got it?"

"Give me a crash course on the laser beam, and I'll be happy to oblige. This other weapon just takes too long. They are on top of me before I can use it."

"No time to teach you now." Roth began her ascent, leaving me to catch up while my hand formed a fist. It appeared that the grenlings knew that she was the more dangerous of the two of us because they did not hesitate to come closer to me once she was further along.

I pointed my hand at one, a midsize creature with a bright orange helmet, and it shifted out of the way just as I was getting to the count of five. When I pointed my hand at it again, it lunged for me before I got to the count of two.

I was only saved from grappling with the creature because I moved my toes down on instinct and shot up, almost overshooting Roth's position before I leveled out beside her.

The grenling landed on the cliff underneath me, its claws scraping against the rock wall as it scrambled to catch up to me while looking warily at Roth. I was just bringing my hand to bear on it again when I pulled the trigger, aiming for its head.

It released its hold of the cliff, tumbling against it as it fell.

That's right, I thought, *it messes with their head even without the five-second wait.* I'd forgotten about that.

"Stay closer," Roth said, "I think they figured out you're a newbie."

"They know the limitations of my weapon and they've seen what you can do, how about you activate the laser, so we take them off guard?"

"It is a delicate thing to learn. I don't have the time. Stop questioning me at every turn or I will leave you behind."

Roth was looking away from me, which was a lucky thing because I was sure the image on my helmet showed my disgruntlement.

We were soon fifty feet from the top. The grenlings were kept at bay only because Roth continued to fire, almost at random, taking down dozens of them in the time it took for us to arrive.

I kept trying to take one down, but they kept moving out of the way before my weapon would activate. Finally, more out of spite than anything else, I selected a grenling that was further back than the others and had a moment of satisfaction when its chest burst open, sending it to the bottom of the ravine.

My sides heaved.

I had gotten carried away. It had not tried to harm me. Frustration with my inability to fight the grenlings in a meaningful way had prompted my action.

I can do better.

Roth slowed when we were five feet from the top of the cliff, she turned to face me, prompting me to do the same without thinking about it.

"Okay," she paused to flip around to fire her laser at a grenling that approached like a giant creeping lizard coming over a rock outcropping. It screeched and fell back, having barely suffered damage to its arm. Roth waited to see if it would make another attempt, but it did not.

"We should expect Camp Myers to be leveled and that the lurkers have the run of the scene." She paused to make sure she had my attention. "Even if that is the case, I'm still under orders to infiltrate and pull out the classified object." She gave me a searching glance, which looked a little strange projected on her helmet. "I recognize you don't trust me and I suspect that's because there are many things I have not told you. And it's going to continue to be like that, but I need your help."

"I'm not trying to get answers to everything right now, I just want to stay alive. You'll have my help regardless. Just teach me how to use some of the other weapons, so I'm not left to rely on hand-to-hand combat."

Roth started to respond and then trailed off. A moment later, she gave a quick nod, almost as if deciding it was not worth it to fight me anymore.

"Fine." There was a pause. "I have now activated the laser weapon for you. It works the same as the other weapon, you hold the same trigger. It will take five seconds to fire."

I frowned, not liking this last bit. "Is that how yours works?"

"No, it isn't. As I've already mentioned, this is a complicated weapon to get right. The slightest bump of the trigger and whatever you are pointing at is gone, ripped in half or burned to oblivion. You must be meticulous when you use this weapon. That's why I put you on the starter weapon first, and its why you still have training wheels."

"It's the exact same weapon as yours, just delayed by five seconds, correct?"

"Yes."

There was a movement from behind and Roth turned. The grenling stopped and crept backward. These creatures were learning. I couldn't help but think again that it would have been a far different experience if we would've been adequately armed to fight them back at camp.

"But I don't have to hold the weapon on my target for five seconds before it works, correct? I can press the trigger, count to four, point it on the fifth second, and it will fire."

"Yes. Ideally, you should have the weapon aimed directly at the target you are hoping to take down the whole time, but that's essentially the idea."

"Perfect." One of the grenlings was getting a little too close, I pointed my hand in its direction and pulled the trigger, it immediately shied away. Rather than following it, I let the weapon hit the rock where it had been. I was satisfied when the laser beam came from my hand, just like Roth had been using.

Nothing happened to the rock, just as before.

"Because this weapon is so dangerous, it has been configured so that that it will only affect living flesh."

Roth had anticipated my next question so I shifted gears.

"I could point it a building, but nothing would happen?"

"Probably. It might be a different story if there's somebody directly on the other side of a wall, they might get burned. For example, if you used that on a tent and there was somebody on the other side, they would be torn in half."

"Let's go," I said with more than a hint of satisfaction at finally having a real weapon.

I had an easier time forgiving Jeffords for never training us on the rifles now that I had access to this.

Things were about to get a lot more interesting.

40

We inched forward to the top of the cliff, moving slowly while the grenlings became restless. They steadily closed the distance, coming out into the open, braver as their numbers increased. They stayed more than fifty feet back and to either side of us, with the one that Roth had turned to deal with hiding behind an overhang that jutted out from the cliff. Those underneath us came even closer. I pegged the nearest one at about thirty feet away. I followed Roth's lead because she was adamant that we could not risk popping over the top. She was concerned that if we moved too fast, even while staying low on the mountain, that we might show up on the lurkers' radar. She hoped to mitigate that risk by using a gradual ascent.

It was easy in theory, but much harder in practice with the grenlings swarming around us. One moved from the pack until it was about fifteen feet away. I moved my hand towards it but stopped from pulling the trigger at the last moment, figuring that Roth would do something about it if she was concerned.

I grunted. "Did you want to shoot him or shall I?"

"Hold off." Roth didn't explain further.

It seemed like it took five minutes, but it was probably far less before we arrived at a point where I could see over the top of the cliff. At first, I could not see much, just more rock, but as we continued up, I could see some of the horizon.

The first things I noticed were plumes of smoke, rising ever higher in the air. Several of the larger lurker ships also hung impossibly in the sky without any apparent force keeping them there.

There was discernible activity below the great vessels, I could mostly just see flashes of light from small streaking ships. Few sounds of the battle made it to us. I figured Camp Myers was at least three miles away.

Roth had a sharp intake of breath. "The battle is still going. This is what I hoped for." She glanced over at me, apparently not recognizing how callous she sounded. "It will give us cover when we get closer."

When we were up high enough that we could skate forward onto the top of the mountain, Roth did just that and landed softly without more than a whisper, turning off her anti-gravs as soon as she was on the ground.

I came down hard when I tried to execute the same maneuver, causing Roth to curse as she glanced over at me with annoyance on her face.

"Quiet."

I didn't respond, but she should expect that my ability to use the suit was still limited, especially since she had taught me nothing on how to land.

I wanted to reactivate the anti-gravs and jump off the ground again, just to see if I could figure out how to land softly but restrained myself. It was difficult that the only practice I ever seemed to get was when I was in the middle of a situation.

"We are going to cross the top on foot," Roth said, "I don't want to risk flying."

"What about the grenlings?" I asked while turning back to look over the cliff. None of them had followed us, but I could hear them moving down below. "It won't be long before they're right behind us."

"I don't know what more we can do about them. Our time is better spent completing our mission. Stay close."

Roth stalked forward. I followed, conscious of the fact that the noise behind us increased the further we went. It would not be long before the grenlings were on top of the cliff as well.

I didn't know exactly what Roth's game plan was, she had not taken the time to explain it to me, but I expected that when we got to a place where we could jump, we would turn on our anti-gravs and descend until we were at a safe height for traveling before flying to the camp.

The top of the cliff was barren, with a few trees that had long since died and had been burned to a former shell of what they must have been by the intense sun.

That's another nice thing about the suits, I don't have to worry about putting on block.

I didn't even know if I still had my block with me and suddenly became afraid that it might have slipped out while I was in the transport ship. The block meant life. I knew that better than any other thing I had learned here. I reached for my pocket but, of course, could not feel anything through the suit.

"What are you doing?" Roth hissed, turning to face me.

I had not realized that in my effort to find the block, I had been making noise by clapping my suited hand against the metal suit.

"I was just checking to see if I had something."

"Stop it."

Roth waited as if for an apology, but I refused to give it. When she resumed going forward, I resisted the urge to keep looking back over my shoulder at the grenlings that were right behind us. As Roth was insistent on not using our weapons against them while up here, it was better to be a little in the dark.

At least for the moment.

We came to a small ravine that was about ten feet across, going as far as I could see in either direction. The inside was full of vegetation similar to what I had seen my first time down a ravine.

Roth activated her anti-gravs. As she skated across, a grenling reached up from within and grabbed her by the boot, pulling her down.

I was just starting to skate across too and pulled to a halt. I could not see where she had gone. It was like she'd been swallowed by a whale in an ocean of green.

"Roth, are you okay?"

No answer.

As a precautionary measure, I brought up my hand and aimed it at the ravine in front of me, my finger playing with the trigger.

She was capable, but the undergrowth was thick. I remembered all too well the many creatures down in the vegetation, and while my suit would probably protect me against them, if there was no need for me to hop down after her, I was eager to avoid it.

I didn't expect that I would be able to see anything down there. Undoubtedly, the suit had other features that would allow Roth to better deal with the situation, but she had not taught them to me.

It's time to stop ignoring the inevitable.

I turned and saw that a handful of grenlings were now up here, crawling forward on all fours as if they were aware of what was happening at Camp Myers but still determined to come after us. I raised my hand and pointed it at them, causing several to scurry back, some even going so far as to return to the ravine.

"Roth, come in."

I heard static. "… I have the situation… Stay… Don't engage…"

Even though the message was garbled, I knew she didn't want me to mess around with the grenlings anymore. They were now less than fifteen feet away and creeping closer.

"Easier said than done. Would it be better if I came down after you?"

"No."

I could not tell if she said anything else as I once again raised my hand and pointed it at the oncoming grenlings. I aimed at one and pulled the trigger, feeling bad for disobeying her order, but also knowing that I could not fight all of them at once. It would be better to pick them off one by one.

They turned and scampered away.

I heard a roar from behind.

41

I didn't know what it was that made the grenlings run away from the lurker—perhaps they understood that these creatures were more technologically advanced and dangerous. As I turned to face the lurker, I suddenly wished that I was facing the grenlings again because I had a better chance of surviving a fight with them.

A solitary lurker had come up from the valley below.

Blasts of light from its weapons hit me and were absorbed by my suit, which flashed each time, making me fear there would be a limit to the number of shots I could receive before it became a problem. A moment later, four additional lurkers rose up to join it. Activating my anti-gravs, I pushed down with my toes and leaped into the air while pulling my trigger before aiming, keeping a conscious count of the seconds as they passed. Roth had warned me against doing this because she feared that I would hit something by accident, but I needed every advantage I could get in the battle in front of me. I took aim at one, but it was still two seconds more before it fired, ripping the creature in half.

"I thought I told you to…" I didn't make out the rest of Roth's words as I twisted my feet around and slid backward and to the side. I was uncertain if it was because she was still breaking up or because I was too distracted by the four remaining lurkers.

"Our precautions didn't work. The lurkers found us."

There was a long pause.

"Say … again?"

This time I could hear Roth more clearly, I knew she had not trailed off because of interference but was still engaged in battle with the grenling that had taken hold of her.

"Five lurkers," I said, "down one."

Blasts of light flew towards me, flying right by my feet as I twisted out of the way, feeling like an Olympic skater who had suddenly been thrust into a dogfight.

I flew towards the closest lurker, pulling the trigger of my hand and waiting for the painful five seconds again before it fired. The lurker twisted out of the way just before my shot would've hit, the blast of light flying harmlessly into the mountain behind it.

"If you're able to activate my weapon so it fires immediately, now would be a great time."

There was no response, and when I pressed the trigger to aim at the same lurker again as I flew past, turning in midair as I did to keep my aim, I could tell that the nature of my weapon had not changed.

I was thinking of going in close again like I had before, hoping that the other lurkers would not shoot if their comrade was in the line of fire. Before I could do that, another came zooming towards me with its blasters blazing, keeping me from executing the maneuver.

I twisted my hand around, pointing it at the lurker and hitting the count of five a moment later. The laser ripped through one of its wings but otherwise did no damage. It only served to make the creature angrier as it doubled its speed, coming at me with its weapons firing so fast it was difficult to discern between the various blasts of light.

I counted no fewer than six blasters in its hands as I spread my feet and dropped almost down to the mountain before correcting and skating forward, all while keeping the trigger of my blaster down and bringing it around at the last moment to aim it at the nearest lurker. This time it was a direct hit.

I got it in the head, sending it spiraling down to the mountain. It made a massive oomph when it crashed.

As I turned, I saw that several of the grenlings were up at the top of the cliff with their heads peeked over, watching the battle. One of the grenlings crept forward and snatched something away from the dead lurker.

It pointed the dead lurker's blaster at me, and despite the small size in the grenling's large clawed hands, it somehow managed to get off a blast. I had already depressed my trigger as I flipped around to point my hand at the grenling. The blast came a moment later, ripping into it and sending it over the cliff with the blaster flying free.

Hoping that none of the other grenlings would be so bold as to try the same move, I turned around just in time to receive a blast in the chest. Like before, the suit lit up, but right afterward, a red flash in the corner of my eye lit up as well.

"Roth, there's a flashing red light in my eye. What's it mean?"

Assuming that it meant the suit's shield was down, I pushed my toes down and shot into the sky, not slowing until I was five hundred feet above the closest lurker. I then pushed my toes open to increase the distance between them and me, lining up my hand with the nearest creature while pressing the trigger. Five eternal seconds later, the laser shot from my hand, ripping into the creature and killing it.

"I only have two lurkers left, but the flashing light is not going away. Please advise."

There was no response.

And both lurkers were angry at how I had taken down their comrades.

From my perch in the sky, I caught a good look at Camp Myers and saw that there were hundreds, if not thousands of suited soldiers fighting with lurkers on the ground and in the air. I only got a glance before I had to engage the oncoming lurkers.

42

Rather than coming at me from below like the others, these two had gone high and came from above. I had not seen them during the last couple of minutes, so it seemed like something they had been working on while I had been dealing with the other lurkers. The flashing light in my eye made me far less cavalier.

"Roth, are you there?"

No response.

I imagined her grappling with the grenling below, and while I doubted the grenling would get the best of her, I needed her help now.

I twisted and turned, skating backward as I did, even though they were not yet firing their weapons. They spread out, first by about twenty feet, but it was soon over a hundred. It appeared they were positioning so they could come at me from two directions at once. I didn't have any idea how much they knew about the vulnerabilities of our suits, but they knew more than I did. They did not seem phased by me or my actions in the slightest, and their approach was methodical.

The ravine below was still as full of grenlings as it had been before. There were no grenlings in the air. They had latched onto the cliff to watch what was happening with me.

Considering how they had scampered away when the lurker had appeared, I was surprised they had stuck around to watch this battle.

I didn't know how the lurkers communicated—from my perspective, it did not look as if they had radio equipment—but when one started firing, the other did too, in the exact same moment.

I spread my feet and dropped, widening them so that I fell faster than the pull of gravity. I was about a thousand feet above the top of the cliff when I started. When I got close to the peak, instead of slowing to go a different direction, I widened my feet even further and plummeted down, disappearing into the ravine in what I hoped would be an evasive maneuver the lurkers would not match.

The grenlings were shocked by my sudden arrival but hardly missed a beat. The ones that could fly launched into the air, I was soon dodging them as well as blasts from above. A hail of boulders came my way as if initiated at the command of a leader. I spread my heels even further as I fell, zooming out of the nasty storm.

I came out of my fall and flew through the ravine at a speed far faster than I cared to think about, while I waited to see how the lurkers responded. Even more grenlings now came after me, throwing clubs and rocks again like they had before, swooping like crazed flying squirrels.

Most of their missiles missed me by miles, but too many came close. I twisted and turned out of the way as best I could, but a basketball-sized rock hit me in the chest, and even though it was smaller than some of the others I had been pummeled with, this time, I felt it.

The red flashing light did not change. I hoped that the suit had not been further damaged by the rock. I was suddenly more aware of the precariousness of my situation. When I turned back to locate the lurkers, they had come down from their perch in the sky but were still out of range of the grenlings.

They were waiting for me to come out of this madness, something I was tempted to do if only that red flashing would go away.

I flipped around, doing my best to avoid the flying grenlings.

It wasn't ten minutes ago, that dealing with the barely sentient monsters had taxed me to the fullest, and now it seemed a far easier thing to deal with these creatures than the lurkers up above.

I could deal with bruises and bumps from the grenling's unsophisticated weapons, but the lurkers could kill me with one shot if I was not careful.

A nearby grenling launched from the cliff as I passed. It missed me by mere inches, twisting so its claws scored the feet of my suit.

I lurched and feared that it might have affected my anti-gravs, but I righted and continued on my way as if I had just come out of some turbulence.

The lurkers now hovered just above the ravine, staring past the swarming grenlings at me. I twisted and turned and dodged and dove, sparing every glance I could toward the lurkers to see what they were doing.

They waited.

Perhaps they wanted to see if the grenlings would get me.

A large stone bounced off my head, jarring me and almost sending me into a tailspin. The grenling that had flung it was getting another ready to send my way. I brought up my hand while holding down the trigger, intending to take him down, but instead, I turned it towards the waiting lurkers and fired off a shot. My laser went right in between them, doing them no harm.

It was apparently the invitation they needed, because they descended into the ravine, firing their blasters indiscriminately.

The grenlings did not fare well and started falling out of midair. One unlucky grenling was hit in the shoulder, distracting him as he was about to land on a cliff, sending him instead careening into it headfirst. I caught a glimpse of him as he fell to the bottom of the ravine, his head crushed. It was not a pretty sight.

By the time the lurkers were down in the middle of the ravine, at about the same elevation as me, the grenlings were no longer flying. I expected the grenlings to disappear, but instead, they took up their chant again, reminding me of some cheesy movie I saw as a kid of people chanting while sacrificing a woman to a monstrous beast.

A cheer came from the grenlings when a blast almost hit me in the head.

I had counted on the grenlings to give me cover, but the lurkers had put a quick end to that.

Even with the flashing red light still glaring in my eye, I charged the lurkers, pushing beyond what was safe as I headed toward them. I had hoped they might forget about me in all the chaos, but if they were determined to follow me, I had no choice but to face them.

I brought up my hand, pressed the trigger, and spread my heels apart so that I lurched forward while adjusting my aim so that my weapon was aligned with the nearest lurker.

When I had turned to face them, there had been a reprieve in their blasts, but they now started up again. I zigzagged as best I could, feeling like I was about to throw up when I took two hits in rapid succession.

My suit flashed as the blasts were absorbed. Instead of having a hole the size of a pumpkin blown into my chest, as I had feared, it seemed my suit's shield still held.

Another flashing red light joined the first in the corner of my eye. I did not know what that meant but assumed the next hit would be my death.

"Roth, I could really use some help," I said, bringing my hand to bear on the closest lurker while pulling the trigger.

There was no response from her.

When my weapon finally discharged, the lurker moved so I hit its wing instead of ripping its torso in two. It stopped using that wing but didn't suffer otherwise.

The other lurker was now fifty feet above my head, its blasts coming dangerously close to hitting me.

I pushed my toes down and zoomed up. Once I was parallel with the creature, I grabbed hold of a wing and mounted it like a horse, my legs spread wide over the creature's thick body. I held onto the wing, brought up my weapon hand, and pulled the trigger, aiming it at the other lurker, which had flipped around to come back at me.

There was a brief pause when I thought that it might not fire at me because of my position on the back of its fellow lurker, but the blasts came, heedless of its companion.

I ducked down using the lurker as a shield while I kept my hand in the general direction of the oncoming lurker, hoping the blasts wouldn't hit me. My laser finally came though—it seemed to take forever—and it cut through the last half of the lurker's body, almost severing its lower abdomen.

The lurker I rode like a horse roared as I brought my hand around to keep it aimed at the now wounded lurker, which had passed by to the other side. I pressed the trigger while ducking to avoid the worst of the enemy fire. Many blasts went into my ride's body, but it absorbed them without a problem.

I counted the seconds and brought my head up right before my weapon was about to fire, adjusting at the last moment to hit the other lurker directly in the head. The laser went from the middle of its head down through the rest of its unsevered body, cutting it in half lengthwise like I was deboning a fish.

I feared it could still fly because its wings worked, but it could not maintain flight and sunk to the bottom of the ravine.

The grenlings shrieked and howled. No fewer than a dozen leaped off, clubs in hand as they descended with bloodcurdling cries.

The lurker's fall seemed to have awoken the grenlings from a trance. They started jumping again, coming for the remaining lurker and me.

It had been my intention to kill this lurker after I had dispatched the other, but I now brought up my hand, pulled the trigger and waited the long five seconds while aiming in the general direction of the flying grenlings. When it finally went off, I was rewarded to see five of them fall out of the air.

Now that was satisfying.

The lurker moved erratically, apparently hoping to knock me free from its back so that it could finish me off. The blasts from its hands were going everywhere as they tried to twist far enough around to get me. I hung on with one hand while pointing my other at another group of flying grenlings. I had pressed the trigger right after I last used it so I didn't have to wait long.

The laser went off, killing at least three grenlings and wounding half a dozen more. Rather than make them back off, it only seemed to infuriate them. More grenlings jumped from the cliff, trying to land right beside me on the lurker. One succeeded, before he had a chance to take hold and sink us, I kicked him off.

The lurker spun in midair and sent me crashing into the side of a cliff. Three nearby grenlings took advantage of the opportunity to leap on top of us. Just like before, only one managed to land.

He was smaller and nimbler than the others, only standing at about twelve feet tall. I brought my hand around and hit him in the face, hoping to knock him off; instead, it grabbed hold of the same wing that I held and headbutted me.

It was more jarring than I expected though it didn't hurt, it forced me to take a moment to recover my orientation, but even as I did I pulled the trigger and brought my hand around, punching it in the face and then holding my hand there until the laser obliterated its head.

It also cut through the lurker, severing a leg and cauterizing the wound in the process. The lurker roared, turning again and knocking me up against the cliff, allowing three smaller grenlings to jump on. The grenlings were fearless, I would give them that.

It was too much weight for the lurker to handle, and we started to plummet.

I pushed the trigger again and held my hand so that it was aimed right at the lurker's head while I kept a close eye on the fast approaching bottom of the ravine. When the laser finally went off, the lurker screamed as its skull was pierced. Its wings stopped working and it fell like a rock.

I released my hold, stood on top of its hardened lobster-like body, and then leapt up, flying into the sky.

The grenlings were still out in full force, but I sped through them like a battering ram, knocking them out of the way, heedless of what it was doing to me or my suit. I was ready to be done with these creatures and unlike before, the lurkers already knew where we were so there was no need for secrecy.

The flashing red lights had continued during this whole time, and thankfully, once I was at the top of the ravine with the grenlings all below me, I had not added any other warnings.

I stopped when I was a hundred feet in the air above the ravine.

Roth had warned me to stay low to keep off of their radar, but it was too late.

I could already see a lurker ship headed our way.

43

"Roth, are you there? We have an incoming ship. We can't waste anymore time on this bunch." I moved until I hovered just over the ravine but received no response. I slowly descended until I hovered an inch above the vegetation.

"Roth?"

Nothing.

I had just started to go into the green depths below when Roth came zooming up, bringing six grenlings with her. I did not have time to jump out of the way before one snatched my foot and fell backward, trying to drag me into the ravine.

I pushed down with my toes and lurched into the air with the grenling holding on. I was surprised Roth had not done something like this when she had been taken captive, but perhaps more grenlings had latched onto her, making it challenging to perform the same move.

"It took you long enough," I said to Roth, who stared at the oncoming ship, "where have you been?"

"I told you to maintain a low profile, couldn't you do that one thing?"

I was taken aback.

She thinks this is my fault?

"I was trying to survive. I didn't go into the air until the lurkers showed up. If you have a problem with how I handled things, you could have come up at any time to help me. I just took down five lurkers by myself, not to mention dozens of grenlings! The least you can do is give me some credit—"

"Credit is for dead men." Her voice was cold.

I ground my teeth as I pointed my hand down at the grenling, pulled the trigger, and waited the obligatory time period. I snarled when the laser finally killed it, causing it to release my foot.

Despite Roth's words of admonition, she was fifty feet in the air. If she was hoping to avoid their radar, she was not doing a good job herself. I came down until we were on the same level.

She was irate, but this was not my fault.

Given how quick the lurkers had shown up after she disappeared, they must have already been on to us. It was that or a patrol had stumbled upon us.

"Maybe if you had given me—"

Roth cut me off. "It was a mistake to give you as much as I did. You just put our mission in jeopardy, soldier. I told you to stay put and to keep your head down, you did neither of those things."

It was difficult to not attack her, but I somehow managed it. Instead, I clenched my hands into a fist, which had a similar effect on my suit. I wanted nothing more than to knock some sense into her.

"I don't know if you noticed, but a grenling just tried to pull me down into the ravine," I said, "all I had to do was put my toes down and I brought it up. You could have done the same thing."

"I was trying to stay off the radar," she said through clenched teeth. "I figured that taking the time to handle the situation, rather than leaping into the air, was the right call. If I would've known how reckless you are, I would've done things differently." She had turned towards me during her tirade, but she now turned back to the oncoming lurker ship, heedless of the swarming grenlings underneath us. They were no longer hiding and seemed to only grow in number as more came up from both ravines.

"You've really messed this up."

I said nothing. I was not going to apologize.

Without another word, she spun while igniting her propulsion and left me in her wake.

44

To: Lieutenant General Regina Adams
From: Brigadier General Katrina Roth
Log date: 00429.211-15:42:19

Re: The asset

General Adams,

The asset is as safe as I can make him for the moment. You will be happy to hear that he is proving himself beyond what we hoped.

Brigadier General Katrina Roth

45

The fury that ran through my veins like burning gas drained out of me as I watched her disappear, moving so fast that the lurker ship did not seem to notice she had left. It did not alter course and still came my way.

I could understand that Roth was mad, particularly because she worried that the mission had been put in jeopardy, but this was not my fault. She should've listened before flying off in a huff.

"Roth, what are you doing?" I asked, not expecting a response but thinking I ought to start up a dialogue.

A memory came back to me of her cackling like a madwoman while shooting grenlings.

There was no response. I spread my heels apart and followed after her, wondering what new madness I would have to deal with now that she had abandoned me.

She was crazy.

I should've expected this, I thought, remembering how she had almost left me to die on the first day we had run from the grenling.

I cursed as I followed after her, leaving the grenlings behind. Once I was clear of the mountain, I adjusted my altitude, so I was only fifty feet above the ground. I then spread my heels as wide as I could. Even though it seemed fast, I was not going to escape before the ship arrived.

And there is no chance of me catching Roth.

It was one of the small lurker ships, similar to what had attacked our camp earlier in the day. I thought it might have held as many as twenty-five lurkers, but that was a guess.

Surprisingly, the ship did not turn to intercept me. It was not until five minutes later that I realized our assessment was wrong. It had not been heading towards us at all, it had been slowly ascending into the sky.

"Roth, it was not coming for us."

There was no response. Even though it seemed like the immediate danger had passed, I stayed at a low altitude, going as fast as I could, while remaining on the lookout for obstacles that cropped up in my path.

I approached a cluster of hills, nothing like the mountains we had just come from, but rather than navigate through, I figured I was close enough now that a solitary figure should not raise much of an alarm, so I just went over.

If Roth has a problem with what I'm doing, she shouldn't have left me to my own devices. I was no longer part of the classified mission, so there was nothing for me to give away.

I looked down as I flew over the hills, scanning to see if there were any grenlings. When I saw movement in a small crevice, I instinctually pushed my toes down and moved up twenty feet before I corrected. I didn't get a good look at the creature, but it was no grenling. If there were any here, they were well hidden.

I was soon past the hills, descending until I was at a height of fifty feet.

Camp Myers was quickly growing on the horizon. Unlike the training camp where I had come from, it had permanent buildings, some were as tall as five or six stories, towering over the surrounding wall that looked like it was intended more to keep local creatures out, rather than help them fight lurkers.

They didn't think the lurkers would find them here, big mistake.

I no longer tried to hail Roth, she was long gone.

Yet I still head towards the battle.

It seemed the most logical thing to do. I still needed a way off this planet, if nothing else.

There were dozens of lurker ships like the one that had left, maintaining an altitude of several thousand feet above everything else. The lurker carriers were above those. There were so many lurkers in the sky that they looked like swarms of dragonflies.

A few minutes later, I was close enough that I decided to slow down and adjust my height until I was only twenty-five feet off the ground, which meant that I now had to focus on my surroundings a little bit more to ensure I did not run into anything.

Surprisingly, and for the first time outside of the mountains, there were actual trees on the ground. They looked like hearty things, a cross between pine trees and cactuses. None of them were taller than ten feet, the majority were far shorter.

I was lost in thoughts of home when I heard something approaching. I stopped and listened but did not see anything on the immediate horizon despite the fact I was twenty-five feet in the air. There were several low hills in front of me that I assumed kept me from getting a view of what was coming. After only a moment's hesitation, I dropped and crouched beside a large boulder. If anything noticed me, hopefully, they would think I was just a discarded suit.

The flashing red lights disappeared while I waited.

I still didn't know what that meant. I had no way of knowing if the shield had reformed or if I would shortly be out of power.

I became angry when I thought of Roth.

I took a deep breath and let it out slowly, trusting that the suit would hide the noise.

The buzzing grew louder, filling me with dread and making me wish for a better hiding spot.

There were several of the strange looking trees in front of the boulder, but they were too short to provide much protection. I crouched down as best I could, feeling like I was painfully obvious to anybody who looked.

The noise was close now.

While doing my best to keep my head down, I shifted so I could look up. Not one minute later, the most massive swarm of lurkers I'd seen yet zoomed by overhead.

It was easily a hundred, probably more. Sweat trickled down my face and back as they passed. It was the first I could recall perspiring during the last several hours, really since I had put on the suit. I had not even thought about it, but I assumed now that the suit had some sort of environmental control mechanism because I had been comfortable while inside of it.

I didn't dare move an inch as the lurkers passed overhead.

They continued by without stopping.

Perhaps it was lucky that they were in such large numbers, as a smaller group might have been more apt to investigate.

All of the sudden, it seemed like the sun was blotted out. At first, I assumed it was another ship, but then I saw it was the largest lurker I had ever seen, easily as large as one of their smaller transport ships. It flew just over the swarm of smaller lurkers, headed in the same direction.

Wherever they were going, they had a purpose. I watched as they left, fearing they were going back to where I had come from to legitimize Roth's abandonment of me, but they took a sharp right and went over the mountain range in a different direction. I just assumed that there was some other human camp over there.

I heaved a quiet sigh of relief. When I ran into Roth again, I was going to give it to her.

I waited until they disappeared before I slowly lifted up off the ground by only five feet and skated forward. I was no longer in the mood to fly any higher. It just seemed too risky.

I hated that my best option was still to head towards the battle.

46

I arrived at Camp Myers ten minutes later. I approached without any problems, skating just a foot or two above the ground while being careful about any obstacles. I had learned the hard way that if I got distracted for just a moment, something could pop up and I would be sent head over tail.

I crouched behind some boulders that still left me feeling very exposed while I tried to get a lay of the land. The walls around the camp were fifty feet tall. I could easily hop over, but I didn't know what I'd find on the other side.

From my perspective here on the ground, it looked like the majority of the battle was in the air, but I didn't want to jump over and find myself in a group of lurkers.

Roth had been afraid the battle might be over before we got here, but as near as I could tell, it looked like it was still hot and heavy. Everywhere I looked, I saw suited soldiers engaged in battles with the lurkers, zipping this way and that, as the lurkers followed after them. There were far more lurkers then soldiers, but it appeared that our suited soldiers were superior to the average lurker. As I watched, one soldier took down three lurkers in a couple moments, all while receiving fire and never slowing in the slightest.

If they'd trained us on the suits, the massacre at our camp could have been avoided.

I hesitated for several minutes, trying to listen to anything that might be close by before giving up and skating forward. I paused again at the base of the wall and listened, wondering if my suit had sensors that could help in my present situation.

I hopped over, watching every which way as I did, fearing that I would draw some lurkers to me. Once I knew it was clear on the other side, I hopped down, deactivating my anti-gravs when I was only a few inches from the ground rather than trying to properly land. The noise of the battle covered the small sound I made.

I was surprised by the number of tents, I had expected more permanent quarters. Camp Myers was set up in the same fashion as our camp, except there were buildings towards the middle.

A suited figure slammed into the wall twenty feet away from where I stood, breaking part of it, but doing less harm than I would have expected. It seemed he had used his anti-gravs to mitigate the damage, both to himself and the wall. Without looking at me, he hopped back up in the air and zoomed away, a lurker following after him.

I had naturally shrunk back towards the wall, but now I forced myself forward.

"Roth, are you here?"

There was no response.

Why didn't I hear chatter from any of the other soldiers?

I had just assumed we were all on the same frequency, it appeared that was not the case. Maybe my transmission to Roth was lost in all the noise.

Or more likely, she just doesn't care what happens to me.

Squaring my shoulders, I walked into Camp Myers, my finger on the trigger, ready to press it the moment I needed it.

47

I crouched against a wall while I watched a suited soldier fight three different lurkers. One was on top of a building, another one was embedded inside, and the third was on the street. All slowly advanced on the man, as if expecting to catch him off guard at some point. He jumped up and down, moving every which way, while somehow avoiding the blaster fire coming his direction. I had a clear shot on one of the lurkers, but up until now, I had not fired my weapon, preferring to stay in the shadows.

The man seemed to be doing okay, although I was a little surprised he had not killed any of them. While I watched, a laser blast came from his hand, but it completely missed the lurker by about five feet. He was already jumping as blasts converged on the spot he had just been.

I caught a glimpse of the man's face on his helmet. He looked younger than me, and judging by the height of his suit, he was far shorter as well. He landed on top of a vehicle I could only describe as a cross between a jeep and a moon lander, crushing the top as he came down, firing a blast at the closest lurker and missing it by two feet.

Blasts came from the lurkers, hitting him in the chest and lighting up his suit. At the rate he was going, he did not have long before his shield would be deactivated and he would be a sitting duck.

The lurker in the street hopped into the air, its buzzing wings echoing off of the walls.

I brought up my hand, pressed the trigger, and pointed it at the lurker's head, maneuvering my aim so that when it fired, it was a direct hit, cutting the creature out of the sky. It screamed as it turned on me and fired off one blast before it died.

This drew the attention of the other soldier and the remaining two lurkers.

I brought my weapon around to another, but it was already firing at me. One blast hit my chest before I jumped into the air and landed on the roof of a building, the metal indenting underneath me as I came down.

I had just jumped over fifty feet without the anti-gravs. I had not known that I could do that.

I brought my weapon around, but the other man had already taken care of it.

The remaining lurker was between the two of us.

Its wings buzzed. I thought it was going to flee but instead it jumped on top of the soldier, smashing him underneath. He had managed to get off a shot before he had gone down, but it had gone wild, careening into the side of the building and doing no damage. I jumped on top of the lurker, grabbing hold of a wing and pointing my other hand at its back while pulling the trigger.

It jumped into the air and spun, trying to ram me into a wall. My weapon finally fired, tearing through its abdomen and up through its head, emptying its guts on the ground. I hopped off as it crashed into a building, knocking down half the wall.

I landed with my trigger depressed and a weapon pointed towards it, but need not have bothered because it too was dead.

I thought about commenting on the soldier's poor marksmanship but bit my tongue.

He probably wouldn't hear me anyway.

"Thank you," he said.

It took me a moment to respond, because I was shocked that I could hear his voice. I saw his lips move on his projected facial image, so I knew that it was him talking.

"You can hear me?" I asked.

"Yeah. I take it you're a newbie." He looked at the dead lurker. "You're not doing too bad if you are."

"I've only been here for like four days."

He laughed. "Nothing like baptism by fire. Thanks for the assist. What outfit are you with?"

The question took me off guard.

"Outfit?"

"You know, what group?"

"They never told me."

"Huh, strange. What camp were you at?"

"I honestly have no idea."

"Seems like they were trying to keep you in the dark. That's all information they tell everybody here on the first day."

"This is a training camp as well?"

He gave me a strange look. "All of the camps are."

I had dozens of questions, but he was already hopping into the air and looking up at the lurkers, obviously itching to get back into the battle.

"Any chance you know how to activate my weapons?"

"You're using your laser just fine, what else do you need? It is the best weapon we have for these things."

"It has a five-second delay."

"Aw, sorry, that really sucks. I can't help you with that, you need to talk to a superior officer."

"She—"

I started to say that she had abandoned me but decided that was probably not the brightest idea. I didn't need him wondering why a commanding officer would leave me behind.

"You want some help?" I asked.

"Sure thing. We have a target-rich environment up there."

"I heard we were abandoning this base."

"More like this whole planet, but why leave any alive if we can kill them?"

"Sounds good to me."

"You got a name?" he asked.

"Anders."

Anderson.

"I'm Smith. James Smith." He hopped into the air while activating his anti-gravs at the same time. I jumped and followed after him, pressing the anti-grav buttons before I dropped to the ground. A small smile flitted across his face when I flew to the left because my toe was out, but he didn't comment on my lack of skill, which was a good thing because I probably would've told him that he was a terrible shot.

He zoomed up at an angle using the suit's propulsion system.

Cursing, I realized that had been a perfect opportunity to see if he could teach me how to use it.

I tried to keep up, but he was already gone. He had just assumed I could follow.

I stopped high in the sky but he had disappeared

I hesitated as I spun around to make sure no lurkers were heading my way.

"James? Are you there?"

No response.

Interesting, he could only hear me when we were in proximity to each other. I could not talk to him again unless I was lucky enough to catch up with him.

I brought up my hand, pulled down the trigger, and took aim at a lurker that had its back to me, but just as the laser was about to fire, another soldier got in the way, so I released it.

"Did you make it here?" Roth's voice was equal measures shocked as well as aggravated, she might have been a little impressed as well.

"No thanks to you."

"Might as well make yourself useful."

"Where are you?"

"There's a big building in the middle of camp, it's six or seven stories tall. You will find me on top. Hurry."

48

I saw the building Roth had mentioned and headed straight towards it. A lurker came right at me, so I bounced up while bringing my hand down to aim at it while pulling the trigger, but I was past it before I could fire the laser.

Releasing the trigger, I increased my speed, hoping to get ahead of it, but it must have flipped around because a moment later, my suit lit up with light as a blast hit me in the back. Cursing, I turned and went down while flipping around and depressing the trigger, bringing my hand up on the lurker. It wrangled out of the way at the last moment, my blade of light going harmlessly into the sky, directly towards one of the ships. I could not tell if it was a hit, but I doubted it would do any damage.

The lurker came right at me as I zigzagged out of the way, several blasts coming close. I pulled the trigger again and brought it around, aiming on count four at the middle of the lurker's body, and this time it was a direct hit. It severed the back half of the lurker's body, and while it had to adjust to keep in the air, its wings were all in the front, so its flight ability was not affected by the wound even though it was having trouble navigating.

"Anders, are you coming?"

"I'll be right there," I said while holding down the trigger again and pointing it directly at the lurker's head as it came straight at me. Not wanting to miss my chance to meet up with Roth, I didn't move to the right or left, choosing instead to absorb the blasts into my chest before the laser finally shot out and tore off the creature's head and ripped down its back.

It was dead, without question.

I was almost to the building when another lurker got in the way.

"Is that you?" Roth asked as it came down like a vicious insect bird of prey.

"You mean the fool that has a weapon that won't fire immediately so he can't deal with sudden problems?"

"I'll take care of the lurker, you just focus on getting here."

I hopped over the lurker while depressing the trigger and aiming for the middle of its body as I zoomed past, hoping I might get it before Roth, but I had no such luck. A moment later, it was right on my tail, firing blasts at me.

I landed on the building with a thud, my feet sinking into the roof by a couple inches and breaking loose some tile. The lurker landed right behind me, doing far more damage than I did, but it was dead, having been shot by Roth.

"You have a will to live," Roth said, "I'll give you that much."

I looked at her, breathing heavily, wanting to rip into her, but knowing that was the last thing I should do even though it would have been gratifying to give in to the urge.

I inhaled deeply. "What do we do next?"

Roth gave me a curious look as if she had expected a different response from me. "It's time for us to procure the package."

She hopped off the building, I followed her.

49

I kept a close eye on the battle all around me while I fell, trying to figure out if we were winning or losing. The soldier I had run into had made it clear that we were withdrawing, confirming something Roth had said as well, but judging by the battle that did not look like it was happening yet.

A ship from our side appeared in the sky, entering through the atmosphere. It was far smaller than the great lurker ships, and it hardly slowed while suited soldiers hopped out. It was surreal to see them hopping out of a ship without a parachute even though I had done the same thing not so long ago. They were each spaced out by a second, putting them hundreds of feet apart from one another as they descended. Moments after leaving the plane, they activated their anti-gravs. It appeared they were organized into squadrons of four because after four had joined up, they flew towards the back of Camp Myers. The next four went somewhere towards the other side, making me think they had assigned areas they were supposed to target.

The suited soldiers flew like small squadrons headed towards their various battle objectives, using the propulsion system I'd seen Roth use.

"What's going on here?" I asked as we fell. "Why are more soldiers being dropped in? I thought we were abandoning this place."

"Not without a fight, we're not. This place is burned now as a training ground, so we have to evacuate all the recruits and find a new world where we can activate and train new soldiers."

You mean kidnap the dead.

"That does not mean we're giving up this place as an outpost," Roth continued. "We are going to fight tooth and nail, and we are going to win."

She said this last part is if trying to convince herself, and I supposed that she probably was because even with the addition of the other suited soldiers, it looked like we were fighting an uphill battle. Our people were vastly outnumbered, a detail I had missed when first approaching the camp.

From the corner of my eye, I caught a glance of some soldiers without suits. One popped up momentarily using their anti-grav boots but then disappeared a second later after using a large weapon to fire a laser at a nearby lurker, sending the creature down into a smoking heap.

"How many soldiers do you think are out there? Suited and unsuited?"

"Not nearly enough," Roth said with a tone that made me think she thought I was asking too many questions. Perhaps it helped that our suits appeared to do a better job of protecting us against their weapons than their armament did of protecting them against ours. Our suits were unnatural, whereas they were born with theirs as far as I could tell.

"The lurkers seem to go down easy enough, is there something I'm missing here?"

"The suit you wear is an expensive thing to make. Most of our soldiers don't have them. I don't know if you've noticed, but there's many men on the ground fighting without a suit. It is just because of a happy set of circumstances that you got trained on one when you did and that you currently have one in your possession. Don't make me regret giving it to you."

"Will do," I said as we cleared the last level. I came to a stop while hovering a foot off the ground. I noticed another handful of soldiers who only wore light protective gear. They had large weapons on their shoulders that they aimed at the lurkers. They were far more careful than those in suits. If they missed, they would have a mad lurker coming their way with little for protection.

A soldier—possibly the one I'd seen before who had been successful in taking out the lurker—hopped up into view again, hovering just above to take a shot at a lurker that headed directly towards us. The lurker flipped in midair and fired off a volley of blasts, obliterating the flying man, his light armor having done nothing to protect him.

The lurker was still coming our way when it was taken out by another laser, I did not see who fired it.

Roth deactivated her anti-gravs, so I did the same. The unsuited soldiers who I'd seen a moment ago had already disappeared. I had not noticed whether they had gone into the building or around. The street had several dead lurkers that I kept a careful eye on while pointing my hand in their direction, afraid they might be playing dead to catch us unaware.

When Roth came to a set of double doors, rather than trying to open them, she just bashed them in and entered, having to duck so her head could clear the doorway. As I followed her, I ducked as well, but my head still hit the top of the door frame and broke free a piece of metal that clattered to the ground.

Roth turned back, a wry smile on her face. "Careful. Not everything in here is made for a man your size."

I looked around the room. Was anything here made for a man my size? Even without the suit?

We were in a long hallway. I stopped at the first door and looked in while Roth went on. It appeared to be an administrative room. There were rows of desks with the same type of computers I'd seen back in my training camp.

The room was empty.

I quickly caught up to Roth as she turned into another room that was outfitted with desks and computers. This room had several offices along the far wall, all of which were empty.

"I would've expected somebody in here to oversee the battle," I said.

"It is typical for marauders that all leadership is in a suit and out among the soldiers. It inspires greater confidence."

Marauders?

Roth strode to the back of the room where there was an elevator, she pushed the button.

The elevator door dinged and opened. Roth stepped inside before turning and holding out a hand. "Wait. Take the next one. This will only hold one suited person at a time. We are going down to the fifth level."

The door shut and she disappeared. I waited for several seconds, and then assumed that this would function like elevators from back on earth, and pressed the button to go down so that it would come back up once Roth got off.

The elevator light lit up.

Then the wall behind me caved in.

50

The lurker appeared to have crashed into the building by mistake, coming through at an angle that put it almost parallel with the wall. It took out the first row of desks. I brought up my hand and pressed the trigger while counting before it rolled out and disappeared into the sky.

I pried my finger off the trigger but kept my hand pointed in the same direction, afraid it might come back for me. I could hear its wings buzzing outside as if it were lurking, waiting for an opportunity to attack.

The buzzing disappeared, so I figured it had left.

Just as I was about to turn back to the elevator, it came in head first, blasters blazing, partially crashing through the wall again, sending pieces of brick and debris at me. I already had my hand back up with my finger pressing the trigger, but before I could get off a shot, the first three blasts from the lurker's weapons went right into my chest, lighting up the suit each time. I had a red flashing light in the corner of my eye by the end.

Cursing, I activated my anti-gravs without thinking and put my toes down, shooting up through the ceiling.

I went straight up to the next floor, tearing through rafters and floorboards as if they were only made of cardboard and paper. I stopped my upward momentum the moment I was through the floor, and hovered a foot above the hole I had just created.

I was in a conference room.

I flipped the conference table out of the way as I moved out from over the hole and turned, expecting to find the elevator right behind me so that I could go down while just ignoring the lurker below, but it appeared the lift only went down because there were no doors up here. I heard the lurker and looked down through the hole in time to see its jaguar like head looking up to see where I had gone.

It roared as I pressed the trigger. I was glad the creature's body kept its weapons away from me, but then it turned and brought up its blasters, firing blindly into the room.

I ducked out of the way.

I was a little surprised at how easily I'd gone through the ceiling. I looked at the wall and figured I could do the same. I couldn't remember if it had been brick, wood, stucco, or something else on the outside. I went through the small window. The wall was made of sterner stuff, but I still broke through with ease, taking much of it with me.

I landed, deactivating the anti-gravs. I held down my trigger as I entered through the hole the lurker had created.

It looked right at me while twisting in the small space to get its blasters angled back towards me. I brought up my hand and shot the laser through its bundle of hands, the beam going out it's back and harmlessly hitting the far wall.

My move had not killed it, but it had severed a couple arms and a leg.

The lurker spun and hit me with a clawed leg, sending me careening into the wall like I was a ragdoll. I went through and landed in the office space I had stopped to look at when first entering the building. As I got up, the lurker came through the wall after me. I had already pressed the trigger but was forced to release it as I dove out of the way to avoid a volley of blasts.

I was back on my feet and activated my anti-gravs. I spread my heels and zoomed into the other room as the lurker spun and followed.

Cursing, I went up the hole in the ceiling and skated backward, so I was looking at the hole while holding down the trigger.

It's head popped up and my laser went off.

This time it was dead.

I counted to five while holding down the trigger and shot it one more time, just to make sure I had really taken care of it, then I floated down through the hole and went over to the elevator.

When I pressed the button the door opened.

Just as I was about to get inside another lurker entered the building through the hole created by the previous one.

I slid over and pushed my toes down so that I shot through the ceiling as it launched something that looked like a bowling ball. I was already through the first floors ceiling and kept going through the next.

The blast wave was barely discernable in my suit, but the building rocked and started to collapse.

51

Fearing that I was about to get pinned down, I spread my toes, and shot through the wall, back first, trusting that the suit would protect me through this maneuver. Contrary to what I'd thought, the building appeared to be holding up just fine, at least on the outside.

"Anders, are you there?" Roth asked as I emerged on the other side.

"I'm here, just dealing with a little bit of—" My suit lit up like it had just been hit by a blast. I turned to see a lurker coming straight towards me from the sky. I pressed the trigger, pointed up, and zoomed out of the way while trying to keep my hand level on the lurker. When it finally fired, it tore the lurker in two.

Finally, a spot of luck.

"Say again?" Roth prompted.

"A pocket of lurkers attacked."

"I'll give you a couple minutes to get it sorted out." Roth seemed irritated by the distraction, but what else could I do?

I opened my mouth to encourage her to go on without me, but I desperately wanted to know what the classified mission was about and had been surprised when she had invited me to join her below.

I was going down if I had to kill every lurker to do it.

I landed again beside where the lurker had created a hole and went through with my finger depressing the trigger. I looked around, but the lurker had disappeared. The building might not have fully collapsed, but most of the walls on the first floor were severely damaged.

My heart sunk when I saw the elevator. It was now twisted metal and broken brick.

Cursing, I slammed the crushed elevator doors with my fist and was surprised when I nearly knocked them free.

Of course.

I reached for the first door and found that I could pull it out with minimal effort. I tossed it back and pulled out the other door as well, heaving it behind me as I looked into the shaft. The elevator itself was gone, I assumed it had gone down to the bottom. The inside of the shaft was caving in. If Roth was going to escape, she needed a way out just as much as I needed a way down. I activated my anti-gravs and slid into the elevator shaft, moving carefully to avoid loosening any more debris before I stopped and hung there, studying the crushed ceiling. It looked like it would hold, but I didn't have high confidence that it would hold for long if the building were to be hit with another bomb.

There was no way the elevator would work again.

I opened my mouth to tell Roth about the damage but decided if I did, she might go on without me. It was best to deliver it in person. I spread my feet and sunk into the shaft, going down as fast as I dared. As I descended, I kept count of the floors and stopped when I got to the fifth. I floated there, thinking at first I should just try to bash my way in before I decided to give Roth warning that I was there.

I tapped on the elevator door, forgetting my own strength and causing the doors to buckle.

"Is that you?" Roth asked over the radio.

"Yeah, there were some difficulties, but I'm here now. I probably have to knock the door down to get in.

Roth cursed. "I take it the elevator is down?"

"Affirmative."

I heard her swear again.

"What did you do up there?"

"Survive."

"I'm out of the way," she said in a brisk tone a moment later. "Do it quick."

I could tell she was frustrated at the delay and the loss of the elevator, but there was not much I could do about any of that now. I kicked the door, and was surprised that it flew into the hallway. It had been more challenging to remove the doors on the first floor.

I entered and looked at Roth.

"I'm here."

Roth stalked away. "Finally."

She stopped at a set of doors at the end of the hallway.

"I would have gone on, but I wanted you to stand guard," she said as a disembodied voice told her she needed biometric identification before she could proceed.

"Look alive," Roth stepped out of her suit and turned to me. "I set up the radio between you and me so that it is always on when suited, but you can talk to people who are not in your suit, just press the button by the pinky of your right hand. Also, you always lock up your suit whenever you get out of it in a combat zone, understand?"

So she could hear me the whole time and just responded when she wanted.

I nodded as she turned to her suit and muttered something, closing it.

I pressed the button. "Are you getting back in your suit before you go inside?"

"No. Don't follow me, at least, not until I give you the go-ahead. Got it?"

"Sure."

Roth frowned at my tone before she put her face up to the door. A bright red light scanned her eyes. A screen to the side flashed green. A rod protruded from the wall that requested a saliva sample, which it processed before the doors opened to let her in.

I was tempted to disobey her order and watch, but she had a tendency to leave me behind without warning, so I decided to not test her. I waited while straining my ears to overhear what was going on inside the room, but heard nothing.

A minute passed, then it was two. I thought I could hear something up above and went towards the doorway, listening at the elevator shaft, but heard nothing more.

Roth called out.

"Be right there." I studied the top of the shaft, wondering what was happening up there.

I realized that I had forgotten to press the button so she could hear me. I pressed it.

"Be right there."

A moment later I stood outside the room. Roth had come out to meet me and muttered something about how I should be out of my suit for this, then shook her head and said something else about not having the time.

"What I'm about to show you is highly classified. I will kill you if I ever hear you mention this. I will knife you in the back with no warning. I won't even think about it afterward and certainly won't feel guilty. Got it?"

I nodded.

"Okay." Roth turned towards the door. "Come here, honey."

A little girl walked out, she wore pink pajamas.

52

To: Brigadier General Katrina Roth
From: Lieutenant General Regina Adams
Log date: 00429.211-18:57:17

Re: The asset

General Roth,

Has the asset been evacuated or not?

I have heard from a little bird that you are undertaking a rescue mission in Camp Myers, I just hope that that you evacuated the asset and did not bring him with you on this ludicrous mission.

Lieutenant General Regina Adams

53

I looked at Roth and had a hundred different questions, but knew I should not ask them in front of the girl. Hope fluttered in the back of my mind because the child made me think of my own son that I had left behind, perhaps it was not so far-fetched to think I might find my family.

A pipe dream.

The thought cut me off guard.

I would not give up.

I will find them.

Another thought occurred to me. *Why did they activate a little girl?*

"I have a hard time understanding why a child would be kept classified." I folded my arms, or at least I tried to, it was not comfortable in the suit, and I soon put them down by my side.

"There are political implications to this that I cannot get into right now, suffice it to say that if her existence is ever discovered, it will cause a war."

"What makes her special?"

"She's special to me," Roth said, dodging the question and putting an arm around the girl as if to protect her. "The peace that we have built with—" Roth abruptly cut off. "All you need to know is that we have to keep her existence quiet. She must survive this attack, and we have to get her off-planet. Can I count on your help?"

"Of course, you don't even need to ask." I shook my head. "But I still don't understand why her existence is such a big deal."

Some of the tension drained out of Roth's face.

"General Roth," I asked, "is this your child?"

Roth glanced back at the little girl, her eyes fluttered, and then she nodded.

"Yes."

I thought back to the doll I had seen poking out of a bag in the general's office and thought it strange that something so innocuous and innocent, could be classified.

How can a little girl threaten so many lives?

DAN DECKER - 201

"I will give you the answers you want," Roth said, noticing my face, "but not here, not—"

An explosion cut Roth off, it was distant, but there was no doubt as to the source. I ran to the elevator shaft and looked up to see a massive fireball.

It was heading our way, slowly but with growing momentum, like a flow of lava downhill.

"Fire," I said. "It's coming down."

Roth paled. "Quick, into the girl's room, it should keep us safe." She added something that sounded an awful lot like, "Hopefully."

The girl had already run inside, Roth was right behind her, and I went in last.

Roth pushed a button and the doors shut.

I heard the roar of fire outside several moments later.

54

To: Lieutenant General Regina Adams
From: Brigadier General Katrina Roth
Log date: 00429.211-19:03:01

Re: The asset

General Adams,

The asset is safe.

Leave it alone.

Brigadier General Katrina Roth

55

The fire went on for some time, raging just on the other side of the door. I put a hand to the metal, without remembering that I was in a suit, but could still feel the warmth of it on my skin. Apparently, the synaptic sense of the suit's hands extended to hot and cold sensations. During all the time I had flown around in my suit, I had not once felt the wind or the burning sun. There was some way the suit distinguished between what it would relay and what it would not. Once the noise of burning fury dissipated, Roth tried to get the doors to open, but they would not work. Smoke came from the screen she had used to control them.

"Out of the way," I said.

Roth curled her arms around the girl and pulled her to the far side of the room.

I tested a door with my fist before giving it a good solid punch, not much happened. I bashed it again and again until I saw light streaming through a crack between the doors. After hitting it several more times, I made a hole big enough that the child could squeeze through. It did not require much more effort to remove one of the doors, allowing me to slide all the way out.

I had been concerned about Roth's suit, but I need not have worried because it appeared to be in good working condition, despite being a little scorched. Her admonition to always close the suit had paid off for her.

"What's the plan now?" I asked Roth once we were outside.

"I don't know. I've never seen anything like that slow ball of fire. I think it's a new weapon."

I looked at the child and wondered if Roth was thinking a nuclear device of some sort had gone off. That would make sense—minus the slow-moving flames—but I hoped that was not the case. If it was, they would be toast anyway because they were already exposed to the radiation.

Wouldn't the suit be smart enough to notify me if there was a problem with radiation?

"Think it was radioactive?" I asked.

"Probably not," Roth said after a hesitation, "it is something else. I assume you don't have any flashing icons?"

"Nothing I didn't have before."

Roth gave me a look. "What?"

"I got hit by a volley of blasts and a red light started flashing."

"And you haven't recharged—" Roth cut herself off. "I didn't teach you about that. The button by your right middle finger recharges your shields, when you press it, the flashing icon will go away."

I pressed the button and the light disappeared.

"Any chance you can disable the five-second delay on the laser?"

Roth gave me a long look and nodded.

"I suppose you have earned that privilege. Hang on."

Roth commanded her suit to open, which it did. It closed around her when she got inside.

The little girl whimpered.

"Don't worry honey, I'll be right out."

Roth got out of the suit a moment later.

"I'm surprised it survived the fire," I said.

"The shields on these are excellent. It will withstand direct contact with a star under the right conditions, at least for a few minutes."

Roth approached until she stood right beneath me, making me feel like a giant who dwarfed her even more than usual.

"I have fully activated your suit. Be careful to not press any of the other buttons until I teach you what they do. I would do that now, but we must go before we have another experience with a new type of weapon."

I pointed at the broken elevator shaft. "Are you going to just hold the girl?"

Roth took one look at her daughter and shook her head.

"Alana is going in the suit."

I gave her a look, forgetting she couldn't see my face without her suit.

"It is engineered to carry a small child," Roth said.

"Why are the suits made for children?"

"You would stop asking questions if you knew what was good for you."

The girl must have understood what her mother was talking about, because she started to whimper. I guessed she was about four or five.

"Don't worry honey, everything will be fine."

I looked over at Roth. "Will she be able to use it?"

"I will control it from my watch."

Roth said something to her suit that I did not catch, the inner mechanisms began to shift.

"Alana," she said, "I need you to come over here and stand by the suit so it can adjust to your size.

The little girl walked forward, bravely looking at the suit while tears trickled down her face. Roth was right by, hand on her shoulder and whispering into her ear while saying words I could not catch.

Figuring I should give the mother and daughter a moment, I walked over to the elevator and looked up at the shaft. I could make out light at the top, which hopefully meant we could get out. At the same time, I was worried about the overall integrity of the shaft.

Debris still fell.

What did the top of the shaft look like now?

I turned back to Roth. "While you get this sorted out, I'm just gonna pop up real quick to look around."

"Wait. We will be ready in just a moment, I don't think it's wise we separate."

I opened my mouth to argue, but she gave me a stern look. I backed down because her daughter was already climbing into the suit. If it looked like it was going to take longer than just a moment, I was going up anyway, regardless of what Roth said. If she had a problem with that, I would remind her of how she had abandoned me.

Twice.

After the little girl crawled into the suit, the straps snaked down around her back and held her like little slings. Once those were in place, the rest of the suit adjusted to give her maximum support, pedestals making up the distance from the suit's feet to her own. After this was done, Roth stepped back and said the words to close the suit.

As she did she wiped a tear away from the corner of her eye and gave me a challenging look as if daring me to say anything, but I just shrugged. I could not tell if that action translated through the suit, so I looked away and made no comment.

Roth soon stood beside me, peering up through the elevator shaft.

"Is there any protective gear you can wear?" I asked.

"Not that's close by, maybe we get lucky and find something up there, but it's unlikely."

I hesitated, thinking of offering her my suit, but if worst came to worse, I was in a better position to make unbiased decisions.

Her girl would be safe enough in the suit.

Besides, my anti-gravs wouldn't work until they were fixed.

Roth brought up her watch and said something I didn't catch while pressing one of the buttons. A holographic display opened up around her wrist. The suit walked over to us after she manipulated something on the display.

"Go into the shaft," Roth said, "but only go up a few feet."

I skated into the shaft and ascended until I was twenty feet up. Roth followed me, using her anti-grav boots as deftly as an Olympic skater.

She ascended until she was level with me and brought out her little girl, keeping her fingers on her watch.

Roth did not have any trouble moving it, though I could not make sense of the controls.

"Are you sure about this?" I asked.

"Unless you know of another way." Roth licked her lips. "Go."

I went up, conscious that the slightest wrong move might send me careening into the top of the elevator and send debris raining down on Roth and Alana. When I envisioned Roth unconscious at the bottom of the shaft, I had mixed feelings about it.

I slowed when I was just one level away from the top and examined the damage. The top of the shaft was not as bad as I had expected.

I peered out at the first floor after I had closed the distance. It was clear, so I slid out and did a quick survey, surprised that the structure still stood after all the damage from the fire. It had harmed everything but the actual structure. I reported back to Roth after I determined it was safe enough.

The desks were gone. The computers had been incinerated, and even the wall separating the two rooms had been destroyed, yet the outer walls of the building remained as they had before, though the paneling on the inside was burned away.

The ceiling had been burned as well. It appeared that the starting point of the fireball had been here, but I could not see what caused it.

Not unless it was an aftereffect of the bomb the lurker had detonated right before I'd gone down. I tried to calculate how much time had elapsed between that explosion and the fireball. I guessed it was ten minutes, possibly more, so that wasn't likely.

Roth slid out with Alana right behind her. After a moment, the suit was back on the floor.

"Try to walk, honey," Roth whispered quietly to her daughter.

Alana took a step, walking with greater ease than I had expected, but that was how it had been for me when I first got in the suit, so I should not have been surprised.

Roth deactivated her anti-grav boots and landed beside her daughter.

"Great job, honey."

I stayed in the air, so I was ready to maneuver if any lurkers showed up.

"I like what you did with the place," Roth said dryly.

"It wasn't this bad when I came down. A lurker set off a bomb just before, it's what destroyed the elevator, but I'm not sure what caused the fireball."

"I may have heard about this. It's supposed to destroy all biological matter in its path, it also takes out electronic equipment as well, though we are not sure why." She bit her lip. "The rolling fire is new. It's like they wanted to make sure to get everything."

"When you say biological matter, you mean humans obviously, trees and plant matter too?" I asked, looking at the walls.

"Anything that wouldn't be classified as rock or metal."

"So this building has become unstable?"

"Probably. It is best to get out as soon as possible."

I headed towards the large opening the lurker had made, as it was closer than the door we had used to enter the building, and peeked out.

The battle was still going strong. Suited soldiers flew through the air, lurkers dove and chased after them, or vice versa, and lasers cut through the sky.

I turned to Roth, who had followed me with her daughter in tow.

"So where do we go from here?" I asked. "How do we get off-planet?"

Roth was doing something with her watch and didn't answer right away.

A moment later she looked up. "There is a transport nearby that is still intact, but I don't like it. It should have been long gone by now." She must have noticed the curious look I gave her because she went on. "All unsuited soldiers were ordered to evacuate an hour ago, and as you and I both saw, there were still soldiers running around down here."

"The transport is broken," I said flatly, "or they would have taken it."

"Most likely."

"How far away is it?"

"Two buildings over." She gave me a searching look. "How about you hop over and find out?"

"You don't want to come with? I thought you said we should say together."

"We'll follow after, but I want you to determine if it's a waste of time or not. And we are staying together, we'll be in close proximity."

"Let's go," I said, trying not to be annoyed as I stepped out and looked around.

A figure walked down the street.

I recognized him.

"Winston?" I called out while pressing the pinky button so my voice would carry.

He turned back but only for a moment.

"Winston," I said again.

He went around the corner, apparently not hearing me over the battle. I hesitated as the ramification of what I had just seen settled down onto me.

Winston had survived the fall or he had been resurrected.

Could Jeffords come back?

I was tempted to dismiss the thought out of hand because I had seen him die, Roth had made sure of that five times over.

But yet…

The thought of Jeffords returning filled me with so much anger that it became difficult to see. I forced myself to focus on the street.

I examined the lurker I had killed before, one of its legs still twitched, but it was dead. I brought up my hand and thought about sending another shot into it just to make sure, but then looked back and decided Alana didn't need to see that.

I crossed to the next building over—it looked unaffected by the battle raging around it—and bashed in the wall, making a hole big enough for Roth and Alana to get through.

I stepped back and surveyed my handiwork. "Roth, how about you guys come over here? It'll be better than waiting in that condemned building."

Roth gave a short nod. "This place is a death trap."

I waited, keeping an eye out as they crossed and entered through the hole. Once they were safely inside, I activated my anti-gravs and pushed my toes down, leaping to the top of the building and hovering just a few inches above the roof.

The building shook.

"Roth, what was that?"

In the distance I noticed that there were no longer just suited soldiers and lurkers in the air, but flying grenlings had joined the melee as well.

Why did they join the fun? Are they still hunting us?

The building underneath me shook again. I turned, wondering if it was an earthquake, but it appeared that the only building that was moving was the one I had just sent Roth and her daughter into.

The other surrounding structures started to shake now too. *Earthquake.*

"Roth, you need—"

A crack formed right under my feet. I forgot I was already in the air and tried to jump, my toes going down and sending me higher before I corrected. I expected the building to crumble, but it followed the crack, separating down the middle. Other buildings along the newly forming ravine did the same.

A large ravine opened.

To my left, a small building was wholly engulfed as it opened wider, far wider than the ravine that had formed the day that I had first met Roth.

I heard cries from the grenlings in the distance.

When I looked down I expected to see grenlings coming up from below, but instead, I saw the most massive monster I'd ever seen.

I thought at first that it was an oversized grenling but discarded the idea. This was something else entirely, a thing that nightmares were made of.

It crawled out of the ravine, passing by me, not even noticing me as if I were as inconsequential as a gnat beside it, which compared to its size, I was.

It towered over the building.

It looked at the battle around it and let out a roar as it fixed its eyes on the lurker ships in the sky. A lurker buzzed by its head, it reached out and flicked it with a claw, severing it in two and sending the remains flying.

"Anders, I need a little help down here!" Roth yelled.

With a final look at the monster, I dove into the broken building, searching for Roth as it bellowed again, seeming to shake everything.

I spotted her perched precariously on the edge of a cliff, trying to scramble back up before she fell into the ravine.

Her daughter was nowhere to be seen.

Before I could get there, Roth lost her grip and fell, knocking her head against a protruding rock.

For a moment, all the anger and fury I had felt at everything that it happened to me seemed focused on this one moment.

I didn't want to kill Roth, but should I keep her from dying?

The question danced in my mind as I watched her fall and heard her plea for help.

Don't be a fool! I thought.

I spread my feet and plummeted after her.

Author's Note

If you would like to receive notifications about other upcoming works, sneak peeks, and other extras, go to dandeckerbooks.com and sign up for my newsletter. Finally, if you would like to reach out, please feel free to drop me a line at dan@dandeckerbooks.com. I always enjoy hearing from readers.

Books by Dan Decker

Science Fiction & Fantasy

Monster Country

Monster Country: Genizyz

Monster Country: Recruit (Novella)

Monster Country: Delivery (Novella)

Dead Man's War

#1: Dead Man's Game

#2: Dead Man's Fear

Red Survivor Mission Chronicles

#1: Red Survivor

#2: The Sawyer Gambit

#3: The Assassin in the Hold

And More!

War of the Fathers Universe

Prequel: Blood of the Redd Guard

Volume One: War of the Fathers

Volume Two: Lord of the Inferno

Volume Three: Enemy in the Shadows

East Wind (Short Story)

The Containment Team

Volume One: Ready Shooter

Volume Two: Hybrid Hotel

Thrillers

Jake Ramsey Thrillers

Black Brick

Dark Spectrum

Blood Games

Silent Warehouse (Short Story)

Nameless Man (Short Story)

Money Games (Short Story)

Mitch Turner Legal Thrillers

About the Author

Dan Decker lives in Utah with his family. He has a law degree and spends as much time as he can outdoors. You can learn more about upcoming novels at dandeckerbooks.com.